The Ordeal of Jason Ord

Also by Lewis B. Patten

GUNS AT GRAY BUTTE
PROUDLY THEY DIE
GIANT ON HORSEBACK
THE ARROGANT GUNS
NO GOD IN SAGUARO
DEATH WAITED AT RIALTO CREEK
BONES OF THE BUFFALO
DEATH OF A GUNFIGHTER
THE RED SABBATH
THE YOUNGERMAN GUNS
POSSE FROM POISON CREEK
RED RUNS THE RIVER
A DEATH IN INDIAN WELLS
SHOWDOWN AT MESILLA
THE TRIAL OF JUDAS WILEY
THE CHEYENNE POOL

The Ordeal of Jason Ord

LEWIS B. PATTEN

DOUBLEDAY & COMPANY, INC.
GARDEN CITY, NEW YORK

All of the characters in this book
are fictitious, and any resemblance
to actual persons, living or dead,
is purely coincidental.

ISBN: 0-385-04486-0
Library of Congress Catalog Card Number 72-97498

Printed in the United States of America

The Ordeal of Jason Ord

CHAPTER 1

I'd been five days traveling across eastern Wyoming, and I still hadn't got nowhere. I hadn't seen another human soul and I hadn't seen a house or even a fence. I couldn't ride no more, because my horse was in worse shape than me, so I walked, leading him.

My name's Jason Ord. I'm sixteen and I was pretty skinny then because food hadn't been exactly plentiful. My hair's the color of fresh-thrashed straw, but it hadn't seen shears for months. My toes stuck out of my wore-out shoes. My overalls had holes in the seat and knees and was frayed at the bottom. My blue work shirt, several sizes too big for me, was whole, but stained with sweat and dirt and faded by the sun. There was half an inch of yellow fuzz on my face, not what you could call whiskers, but what might eventually turn into them. I had a hat, but it was shapeless from being wet so much and you couldn't tell what color it once had been.

Old Nick, my horse, plodded along with his head down. He was bony and swaybacked and twenty years old if he was a day. You could count every one of his ribs, and if you'd a been a mind, you could of hung your hat on his protruding hip bones. Old Nick wasn't poor because of lack of feed, because the grass was knee-high here. His trouble was that most of his teeth was gone and he couldn't chew the stuff.

Sixteen I was, but it had been a long time since I'd thought of myself as a boy. Not since I'd run away from home, dodging sheriff's deputies looking for runaways, riding freights, hiding by day and traveling by night. I'd eaten raw eggs still warm from the hens' nests, and raw turnips, and anything else I could get my hands on. But never had I spoken to another human being and never had I let myself be seen. By God I wasn't going back. My pa had beaten me for the last damn time.

Near sundown my horse laid down. He rolled over on his side with his head layin' on the ground and he closed his eyes. I got hold of the bridle reins and pulled, trying to get him up. I pulled so hard that both reins broke and I sat down hard. They was just so cracked and old they couldn't stand nothing any more.

I felt like bawling but I was damned if I was going to. I kicked the horse, but he didn't stir and he didn't make a sound. His death came easy and quick. He just quit breathing and laid there like a lump.

The saddle wasn't really worth taking off, let alone lugging, but it was all I had except for the clothes on my back. I unbuckled the cinch and pulled until I had got it out from beneath the dead weight of the horse. I looked at the horse and I looked around at the million miles of nothing but waving grass and I was scared. I sat down on the horse's rump. It came to me then. I was going to die too, just like old Nick had died. I'd just lay down sometime, and close my eyes, and die. I didn't have nothing to eat and I hadn't had nothing for days. Nick could've eaten the grass except for his teeth. I couldn't eat it because humans can't live on grass.

I'd lay down and die and maybe nobody would ever find me at all. Coyotes and wolves would scatter my bones and after a while there'd be nothing left big enough for anyone to find. It would be like I'd never lived at all.

I got up. I was damned if I was going to just quit the way old Nick had. I picked up the saddle and threw it over my shoulder. I didn't bother with the bridle. The saddle was awkward to carry but I was damned if I was going to leave it behind. I guess I had some idea of being a cowboy and I knew you had to have a saddle before you could. Besides, a man had to have something—something more than the rags he wore, even if it was only a cracked and worthless saddle with a frayed and worn-out cinch.

The sun went down. The high clouds turned pink and gold but I wasn't noticing. I kept going until it was too dark to see and then I stopped. I had no matches and there wasn't nothing around here that would burn anyway.

I had a thin, ragged blanket behind my saddle and I had the stinking saddle pad. I covered myself with the blanket and put the pad over that and tried to sleep. I couldn't. I just stared up at the millions of shining stars. I ain't never felt more alone than I did that night. I was scared of dying but I made up my mind I was going to die like a man and not like some sniveling, snot-nosed kid.

I got to thinking that maybe if I hadn't been so scared of being caught and sent back as a runaway I'd have been better off. I could of asked at farmhouses for food. I might of been able to get myself a job. But it was too damn' late for maybes now. It was too far to go back the way I'd come, and I knew this empty grassland could stretch on for a good many more days with never a house or a human being in sight. I wasn't going to make it. But neither was I going to quit.

I finally went to sleep. Maybe it was weakness that made me sleep so late in the morning or maybe it was just that I knew there wasn't nothing better to do.

Anyhow, when I did wake up, I was looking up at a man sitting on a horse and staring down at me. For a few minutes neither one of us said anything. I was too surprised. Maybe the man was as surprised as me.

He was an old man, with sun-baked skin that was crackly like paper and covered with freckles that were darker than the rest of it. He must of been at least seventy-five, or maybe he only looked that old because life had been hard on him. His eyes were a funny shade of gray and his mouth was thin and straight.

His cheeks were gaunt and hollow and his face was covered with several days' growth of whiskers. At last he asked, "What in tarnation are *you* doing here?"

I said, "What does it look like I'm doin'? I'm travelin'."

"Away out here? Without a horse?"

"Horse died yestiddy."

"Well I'll be damned! You a runaway?"

I lied, "No sir. My folks is dead."

"Like hell they are! But never mind. I ain't goin' to turn you in. I run away from home myself when I was younger than you. Got tired of the old man beatin' hell out of me. Got tired of workin' for him like a dog an' lookin' ahead an' seein' nothin' but more of the same damn' thing."

I got up, feeling dirty and grubby and brushing the dirt off my clothes. The old man said, "I'm Jim Hunnicutt."

I wiped my hand on my pants before I reached up and

shook hands with him. I said, "Jason Ord." His hand was warm and he had a firm grip, but he didn't try and crush my hand. He asked, as he let loose of my hand, "Hungry?"

"Some."

Mr. Hunnicutt hipped around in his saddle and took a bundle wrapped in a flour sack out of one of his saddlebags. He tossed it down and I caught it. He said, "Cold meat. Cold sourdough biscuits. You dig in. Got a canteen of water here too."

He dismounted and got the canteen from the other side of his saddle. He uncorked it and handed it to me. I already had the bundle spread out on the ground and my mouth was full.

Mr. Hunnicutt hunkered down across from me and rolled himself a brown paper cigarette. He cupped his hands around a match to shield it from Wyoming's everlasting wind. He studied me as he smoked. Finally he said, "Had a boy myself once. Died when he was near your age."

"What happened?" It's a wonder he could understand me with my mouth so full.

"Smallpox. Hit hard around here maybe fifteen-twenty years ago. When you get my age; sometimes you forget."

I didn't know what to say. Mr. Hunnicutt didn't seem grieved to talk about his son's death, but maybe that was because it had been so long ago. He seemed to want to go on talking and I sure didn't mind listening, it being so long since I'd heard any voice but my own.

Mr. Hunnicutt said, "Had it to do over, I'd do different."

"Do what different?" I asked.

"With the boy. I was fightin', then. Fightin' to build this ranch an' hold it agin' them that'd take it away from me. Didn't have no time for the boy. Always figgered when he was growed he'd work with me an' then I'd get to know him an' him me. Only he never got growed up." The old man was silent for a while. Finally he said, almost regretfully, "Had it to do agin, I'd spend time with him from the time he was able to walk."

I drank some water from the canteen. I said, "Guess I'm eatin' like a pig. It's just that I ain't et in about three days. Didn't have too much then. Couple of raw eggs an' some bread."

Mr. Hunnicutt said, "You eat. Eat it all. Only don't eat too fast or you'll puke it up an' it won't do you no good."

I went on eating, but more slowly now. Mr. Hunnicutt said, "My boy's ma took his dyin' purty hard. Moped around six months or so. Then she just up an' died too, in her sleep."

I said, "I'm sorry." I wasn't. It didn't mean nothing to me. But I wanted to be polite.

He didn't seem to hear. He said, "Don't know why I'm runnin' on like this. Don't, usually. Maybe you reminded me of him."

I asked, "Whereabouts is your ranch?"

"You're on it. Been on it two, three days I reckon."

"The house, I mean. Where's that?"

"Main house is south six-eight miles. There's line shacks at the corners. There's a few more houses here an' there where the married help stays. An' the old place where me an' Mary lived when we first come here. Sod, that is."

I finished the meat and bread and washed it down with water from the canteen. Looked like I wasn't going to die, right soon anyway, but I was still a long ways from anywheres. I asked, "Which way's the closest town?"

"Cheyenne's southeast of here, mebbe fifty-sixty miles."

I picked up my saddle. I handed the canteen and flour sack to him. "I'm obliged," I said.

"You ain't figuring to walk all the way to Cheyenne?"

"Reckon so."

"Well I'll be damned! What you goin' to do in Cheyenne?"

"Get me a job."

"What kind of job?"

I said, "I don't reckon on bein' choosy. Any old job that I can get."

Mr. Hunnicutt stared at me. He said, "I'll say this, you got sand in your craw. You want to work for me?"

I stared at him, suspicious now. "You ain't just fixin' to hold onto me 'til you can send a letter to the sheriff back home?"

"Hell, boy, I don't even know where you come from. Besides, I told you I was a runaway myself."

I nodded my head. "All right." I still wasn't sure. I asked, "What kind of job you want me to do?"

"You be chore boy to start. You do everything anybody tells you to." Mr. Hunnicutt mounted. He seemed to know the saddle was important to me. He said, "Hand up your saddle. Then you put a foot in the stirrup and swing up on the horse's rump."

I did, and the horse moved away, heading south. After a while Mr. Hunnicutt asked, "Know how to milk?"

"Yes, sir. I know. But how come a big ranch like yours would have cows to milk? I thought cowboys hated milkin' cows."

"They do. We only got one. My woman likes the milk."

"I thought you said . . ." I stopped. I hadn't no business askin' questions of this man.

But he didn't seem to mind. He said, "Married agin'. Young woman."

The horse trotted and I jolted up and down on his rump, afraid to grip too hard with my legs for fear I'd flank him and he'd buck both of us off.

Mr. Hunnicutt didn't talk, and I didn't mind. My mind was busy, though. I was wondering, if Hunnicutt had such a young wife, why he was out here alone with three-four days' growth of whiskers on his face.

But if he owned all he said he did and wasn't just some old windbag from town, I could see why any woman, young or old, would want to marry him. He wasn't going to last forever and when he died it all would belong to her.

But that wasn't my business either. It was enough that I was riding, that my belly was full and that I had a job.

One thing was sure. Hunnicutt had saved my life. I made up my mind I'd work hard for him. I'd be the best damn' chore boy he ever had.

I had no way of knowing then that I was riding into the damnedest mess any kid of sixteen ever got hisself into. And I had no reason to believe that a week from now I was going to be running for my life.

Not even a little twinge of uneasiness warned me. If it had, I'd have got off Hunnicutt's horse and started walking toward Cheyenne.

CHAPTER 2

It turned out that Hunnicutt was all he said he was and more. His ranch house was three stories high, with scroll-work at the eaves and arched, stained-glass panels all over the windows. The whole thing was white and there must have been twenty or thirty rooms, I guessed. It turned out there was twenty-one.

Out in back of the house was the biggest barn I'd ever seen, painted red, and not far away was a bunkhouse, about three times as big as the average house. There was fifteen or twenty other buildings, ranging from an icehouse made out of logs, to a white-painted, frame chickenhouse with a couple of hundred white chickens scratching around in front of it. The corrals was as big as the ones you find in most railroad yards, with long alleys and pens for separating bunches of cattle into those Hunnicutt wanted to ship and those he meant to keep.

A man came out of the back door of the house as we rode in, and Mr. Hunnicutt named me to him, calling him Red. Red's name was Donahue and he was Mr. Hunnicutt's foreman, which accounted for him being in the house, I supposed. He spoke respectfully to Mr. Hunnicutt and told me to slide off and come to the bunkhouse with him. Mr. Hunnicutt told him to see to it I got something to eat from the cook and that I shouldn't have to do no work until tomorrow.

Mr. Donahue took me to the bunkhouse and gave me a bunk. He told me to wash and he'd go back to the cook and see if there was something hot that I could eat.

There was a pump and a long iron trough on one side of the bunkhouse. There was half a dozen washbasins hanging on nails, and soap on a shelf. I washed, for the first time in at least a week, and dried on one of the dirty towels. Then I went the way Mr. Donahue had gone, and came into a big dining hall, with tables running the length of it and benches on either side. The cook was a Chinese named Sam Wong. He grinned at me and gave me a big plate of beef stew. Donahue disappeared.

I was just finishing, when a woman came. She had an armload of clothes. She laid them on the table beside me and stood there looking down at me.

I knew she was Mrs. Hunnicutt. At my age I considered her an older woman, because she was close to the age Ma was, though she hadn't aged the way Ma had. Her hair was black and done up in a bun at the back of her neck. Her skin was white and her mouth full and smiling and she wasn't thin the way Ma was. She said, "Jason, Mr. Hunnicutt asked me to bring you some clothes. These belonged to his son." She kept looking at me and smiling and all of a sudden I got a funny feeling of uneasiness. I looked down at my plate and said, "Thank you, ma'am. I reckon I sure need some."

I could feel her eyes on me and I don't know why, but I began to feel hot and my neck began to sweat. I supposed I was getting red. She laughed and said, "You'll want a bath. There are tubs in there." I looked up and she was pointing to a door opening off the hallway between the bunkhouse and the dining room.

She stood there a few minutes more, but I didn't look up at her again. I didn't know why she made me feel the way she did, but I didn't like it and I wished she'd go away.

She said, "If you're going to be doing the chores, Jason, we'll be seeing a lot of each other. I hope you'll like it here." She went away, leaving behind the smell of her perfume. My ma had never used perfume and I'd supposed only saloon women did, but it looked like I'd been wrong.

I finished eating and picked up the clothes. I went into the room she'd pointed out. In one corner was a big cast-iron stove. Washboilers for heating water hung on nails next to it. There was four bathtubs in the room, made of cast iron too. And there was another pump and trough like the one out in the bunkhouse. I realized that the trough in the bunkhouse and this one was just separated by a wall. The two pumps wasn't no more than three feet apart and drew water from the same well.

The stove was cold, so I filled one of the tubs about halfway with cold water. I was used to taking baths in cold water so it didn't bother me. I took my bath and got dressed in some of the clothes she'd brought to me. Mr. Hunnicutt's son must have been the same size as me as well as the same age, because they fit. Even the boots fit. They had high heels and looked expensive. I didn't know what else to do with my own clothes, so I washed them in the bathwater and hung them up to dry on a nail over my bunk.

The only thing of my own I still wore was my hat. I went out into the yard.

A man was working in the blacksmith shop, shoeing a

horse. I went in and watched him and pretty soon he stopped and said, "New, ain't you, son?"

I nodded. "Mr. Hunnicutt said I could be the chore boy."

"Then work this bellows for me."

I stepped over to the bellows. I'd done it for Pa, so I knew how. It wasn't hard work and it was pleasant watching the blacksmith heat and shape the shoe. He quenched it finally, and nailed it on. Then he started on another one. But first he packed a pipe and lighted it. "Where'd he find you?" he asked.

I said, "A few miles north."

"What was you doin' there?"

I said, "Travelin'."

"Travelin'?"

I said, "What's wrong with that? People do it all the time."

He grinned. "No call to get feisty, son. If you're a runaway, that's your business an' Mr. Hunnicutt's. But he won't be the one to turn you in."

I said, "I didn't mean to sound feisty."

"Forget it," he said and went back to work.

The blacksmith had finished shoeing the horse and told me he was through with me when I saw Mr. Hunnicutt coming across the yard. He said, "Come on. I'll show you around."

I followed him and he showed me every one of the buildings and told me what it was for so I'd know if someone sent me there. By the time he was through, the noon dinner bell was ringing.

We was right up by the house and Mr. Hunnicutt went

in. Before he did, he told me to go to the bunkhouse and eat with the men.

I heard him say something to someone inside, low enough so I didn't make out the words. Then I heard Mrs. Hunnicutt's voice answering. I was heading across the yard by then and didn't understand her words either, but her tone was something you can't mistake. She was irritated and cross and she was talking to Mr. Hunnicutt the way Ma had sometimes talked to me, as if I didn't have good sense. I thought that if she talked to him that way all the time it wasn't surprising that he spent as much time away from home as possible.

There was only seven or eight men at dinner and I didn't eat much because I'd eaten just a little while before. The blacksmith, who sat next to me, told me there was more than thirty men working for Mr. Hunnicutt, but that a lot of them were out working cattle and wouldn't be back much before dark. Some stayed at the line shacks, riding line to push strays back onto Hunnicutt range because they didn't have fences here. They wouldn't be coming in at all.

There wasn't nothing to do in the afternoon, but I didn't want to sit around doing nothing while everybody else was working. So I helped the blacksmith, whose name was Ike. He didn't say what his last name was and I didn't ask. About an hour after dinner, Mr. Hunnicutt came out, got himself a fresh horse and rode away. Not long after he went out of sight over the horizon, Red Donahue crossed the yard, knocked and went into the house.

Ike's expression as he watched was disapproving, but he didn't say nothing. And while I was only sixteen, I wasn't a complete damn' fool. Several things was plain, even to me and even considering the short length of time that I'd been here. Mrs. Hunnicutt was too young for her husband and wasn't very nice to him so he stayed away as much as he could. The foreman, Red Donahue, spent a lot of time in the house, but only when Mr. Hunnicutt was gone. Maybe that was why she was so mean to Mr. Hunnicutt, I thought, so he'd stay gone and Donahue could be with her.

Well, I guess there ain't much use in dragging this story out. I went to work and I worked as hard as I could, doing everything everybody told me to and doing it the best way I could. I was used to working hard and at least, here, I wouldn't get beat and I'd get paid for what I did.

Mr. Hunnicutt came and went, but in the next week, I didn't see him but twice. Until the last night, anyway. Donahue never left the ranch headquarters, and he spent a lot of time in the house. Once I saw him coming out at daybreak, when I happened to be up a little before any of the other hands. I felt sorry for Mr. Hunnicutt, but I was smart enough to know there was nothing I could do about what was happening. I guessed when an old man married a young wife, this was likely to happen to him.

I couldn't feel any respect for Red Donahue and I guess it must have showed, because he seemed to take a dislike to me. I'd ducked back the morning I saw him coming out of the house, but it was possible he saw me and knew that I'd seen him. He didn't say nothing to me, though, other than to tell me when he wanted something done.

That last night, I went to bed the same time the others did. The lamps went out and after a while somebody began to snore.

I slept. I don't know what time it was when I woke up,

but I had to go to the outhouse. I got up and felt my way out of the bunkhouse in my underwear and bare feet.

There still was lights on up at the house, one in the kitchen and one upstairs. The light upstairs went out as I went into the outhouse.

I sat there with the door open, looking toward the house. I saw a shadow cross the lighted kitchen window. It was a man on a horse and right afterward I saw the square of light as the kitchen door opened. It disappeared as the door closed and the light left the kitchen. It dimmed as the lamp was carried up the stairs, then reappeared in the same window where the light had just gone out.

I heard voices then, shouting voices, and the shrill scared voice of a woman. I finished in the outhouse and headed back toward the bunkhouse. The light appeared in the kitchen window again.

I started to go into the bunkhouse, but stopped with my hand on the doorknob. I thought I'd heard what sounded like a shot, even though it had been muffled, probably by the walls of the house and the closed kitchen door.

I just stood there for a little while, wondering what I ought to do. I should have gone into the bunkhouse and gone back to bed. I should have shut my eyes and ears and pretended I hadn't heard nothing at all. But even considering all that happened later I can't say I wish I had.

So instead of going into the bunkhouse, I crossed the yard and looked into the kitchen window.

Donahue was standing in the middle of the kitchen, holding a gun in one hand and his holster and cartridge belt in the other. He was wearing only his underwear, long red flannels like what I had on. A little smoke still came from the barrel of the gun.

Mr. Hunnicutt was on the floor, lying on his back. I couldn't tell if he was dead or not, but I could see a lot of blood on the front of his shirt. Mrs. Hunnicutt was wearing a long white nightgown and her hair was down, reaching almost to her waist.

Well, I knew there was going to be hell to pay if they caught me there so I backed away as quick as I could.

It was my tough luck that there was a pail on the ground behind me that somebody had left lying there. I fell over it making enough racket to wake the dead.

I knew I was going to be caught and I knew if I didn't get away, they'd kill me too. The kitchen door slammed open and I streaked for the horse Mr. Hunnicutt had ridden here. He wasn't even tied, just standing there with his reins trailing on the ground.

Looking back as I rode away, I saw Donahue raise his gun. Mrs. Hunnicutt came from behind him and put her hand up to stop him from firing. I kicked my bare heels against the horse's ribs and made him go as fast as I could.

The light in the kitchen doorway was hardly more than a dot in the blackness of the night when I heard screaming and then some shots. Right afterward I heard dimly what sounded like a man shouting.

I was worse scared than I'd ever been, but scared as I was, I understood the reason for the delay. Donahue had gone to get his clothes upstairs. He had to be at least partly dressed and they had to work out some kind of story between them that would sound logical.

And I understood something else. I was being blamed for killing Mr. Hunnicutt. What they'd use as a reason, I had no idea. What I did know was that every man on the Hunnicutt ranch and others from the nearest town were going to be after me. And here I was, in my underwear, without clothes or boots and without a gun. I'd thought I was bad off when Mr. Hunnicutt found me. I was a hell of a sight worse off now.

CHAPTER 3

The lights back at ranch headquarters finally disappeared as I went over a high piece of ground. I was cold now. I felt behind Mr. Hunnicutt's saddle to see if any blankets was there. I found some and there was probably a bundle of food in his saddlebag the way there had been the day he picked me up. I didn't even take time to untie the blankets, though, because I could stand the cold a lot better than I could stand being caught.

For the first time, I wondered why Mr. Hunnicutt hadn't put his horse away when he came home. He must have known what was going on, I decided. He must have known all along and had just tonight decided to do something about it. That would explain his leaving his horse just outside the door. It also would explain his going straight upstairs. I thanked God he *had* left his horse standing outside the door.

Speaking of God, I figured I was going to need Him now more than I ever had before. My folks hadn't been church people, maybe because they couldn't even afford what it takes to go to church. Or maybe they hadn't gone because they felt they couldn't dress the way the other people did. I'd seen the church in town, though, and when I was little Ma had tried to teach me about God. She said He wasn't somebody you could rely on to help you every time you needed help. You had to rely on yourself first, and turn to Him only when you couldn't handle it yourself.

I tried to make my mind start working. Up to now, I'd done everything out of pure panic because there hadn't been no other choice. Now I realized that if I was going to get away, I was going to have to use my head.

Even in the dark, they'd follow my trail by lantern light, trying to find out which way I'd gone. Some of them might try catching me by riding in that direction as fast as they could go.

The thing for me to do, then, was to go another direction after I'd given them enough trail to make them think I wasn't going to. So I rode straight for half an hour or so before I turned aside.

When I did, I turned at right angles to the way I'd been going, which had been north. I headed west.

No matter how I tried to control myself, now and then panic nearly overcame me. What if they caught me? What if they made the charge of murder stick? I'd be hung for killing Mr. Hunnicutt who had saved my life and who had been the only person I'd ever known that had treated me decent. They'd probably say I'd tried to rob him, and that he'd caught me in the house. Or, worse, they'd say I had been after his wife and he'd caught me doing that. Maybe everybody would know different, but Mrs. Hunnicutt owned this big ranch now and nobody was going to dispute the word of a woman who had thirty men working for her, who owned near half of Wyoming and had fifty thousand cattle wandering across her land.

I was shivering so bad that I couldn't think of anything except how cold I was. I stopped long enough to untie the blankets and get warm. It was a good thing I did. The horse was lathered and breathing hoarse and hard. If I didn't let up on him, I'd kill him and then I'd be out here helpless, just waiting for them to catch up with me.

I gave him a full half hour to rest while I sat on the ground, huddled in the blankets and wondering where the hell I was going to get some clothes. I didn't have any money and I didn't see how I could get any unless I was willing to sell Mr. Hunnicutt's horse. I wasn't, but even if I had been, I knew it would be impossible. His Lazy H Cross brand must be known all over Wyoming. The minute I tried to sell the horse, whoever I tried to sell him to would know I had stolen him.

Finally I decided the horse had rested enough. I got on again and rode out, still heading west. The sky in the east began to get gray, and pretty soon it was light enough to see.

I got down again. There was a rope hanging from the saddle, and in the saddlebag there was a picket pin. I pounded the picket pin into the ground with a rock and staked out the horse. I took the saddle off so his back would cool and sat down on the ground. I kept looking around like I expected to see a posse galloping toward me. Nothing showed up, though, and finally I stopped looking and went through the saddlebags for food. Sure enough, there was a package of meat and stale biscuits, wrapped in a flour sack. I began to eat, but I only ate half of what was there because I didn't know how long it would be before I found anything else to eat.

I put back what was left. Then I commenced looking through the saddlebags for money. I felt guilty doing it, but I had to have some money.

I didn't find any. I guess Mr. Hunnicutt had carried

what he had on him or maybe he was so well known he didn't need to carry it. I did find a small Colt's pocket pistol and I found a piece of paper and a pencil stub. The paper had been written on and I read laboriously what had been written. *To whom it may concern: Since my wife is a faithless harlot and carrying on with anyone who will have her, I hereby specifically disinherit her and leave the Lazy H Cross ranch and all my cattle and worldly goods to Jason Ord, who reminds me of my son.* Underneath it was signed, *James Hunnicutt.*

Well, nothing could have surprised me more. He'd saved my life and been good to me but he hadn't known me more than a week. He was either clear out of his head or else he was so damned mad at his wife that he'd do anything to keep the ranch from her.

I wasn't a complete fool, though, in spite of my ignorance. I knew a will had to have witnesses. I also knew that I had about as much chance as a snowball in hell of making anybody believe Mr. Hunnicutt had really written it. Besides that, if they hanged me for killing him, I couldn't inherit nothing.

To tell the truth, I never even considered seriously that I could inherit what he had tried to leave to me. It was too unbelievable even for daydreaming.

But I began to think that maybe I owed Mr. Hunnicutt something. He had saved my life. He'd been good to me, even if I hadn't seen much of him. I think he'd compared me with his son. I knew who had killed him and if I could I had to see that his killer paid for what he'd done.

Saying that and doing it were a couple of different breeds of cat. Right now my main concern was saving my neck. That meant getting far away from here. It meant changing the way I looked as much as possible. It meant finding me a place to hide.

But where do you hide in a million square miles of flat prairie land? Sure, there were hills and gullies and even rock outcroppings and low flat-topped hills, but so far as I knew there wasn't any real mountains and there wasn't any real timber.

I rode straight west for a good part of the day. I stayed in the low places as much as possible. I suppose I just kind of sensed that if I rode along the ridgetops I could be seen for miles.

Besides that, being a fugitive and keeping from being seen wasn't exactly new as far as I was concerned. I'd been doing it ever since I'd left home. The only difference was that now I figured I had to travel in daylight whether I liked it much or not. Sooner or later they were going to pick up my trail. When they did, I had to be far enough away so that they couldn't catch up with me.

The land didn't change much except that once I sighted some mountains toward the south. I wondered whether I ought to head for them and try to hide. Then I decided against it. I still wanted a lot of distance between me and them I knew would be following.

I don't know how far I had traveled. I didn't know what time I'd awakened last night or what time I'd ridden away from Mr. Hunnicutt's ranch. I guessed the distance I'd covered at forty or fifty miles.

At least I was off Hunnicutt range. And if I stayed free another day and night, I thought I might have a chance of getting clear away.

Toward late afternoon, I came over a little rise and saw a shack in the gully ahead of me. It was made out of sod cut out of the prairie, laid up like bricks. It had a flat roof, with sod laid on top of it to keep the rain from coming through. The poles stuck out in front to make a kind of porch.

There was a corral down in a dry wash back of the place and I could see cattle in it in spite of the way it seemed to be hidden. I rode closer and saw a rifle barrel sticking out of one of the windows where the glass had been knocked out.

I stopped. I didn't know what else to do. If I kept going I was afraid I'd get shot. I waited for what seemed like an awful long time and then the rifle barrel disappeared. The door opened and a man came out, the rifle still in his hands. He was looking beyond me and when he got out away from the cabin he searched the horizon on all sides of him.

Well, I sure wished I had something on but my underwear. He beckoned me and I rode toward him. He was lean and bony, but the kind that was all muscle and sinew. He was about Pa's age, and he reminded me of Pa. He had a pair of the coldest eyes I had ever seen, kind of greenish, and his mouth was just a slash in his face. There was several days' growth of whiskers on his face. He wore pants, and scuffed, run-over-at-the-heel boots, but no shirt, only the top of his underwear above his pants. A gunbelt was buckled around his waist and it held a revolver with walnut grips.

He said, "Well I'll be damned!"

I didn't know what to say so I didn't say anything. I didn't know what I wanted from him. Maybe only clothes.

He said, "What in the hell are you doing out here in

nothin' but your underwear an' ridin' old man Hunnicutt's horse?"

I said, "I ain't going to tell you. But I need some clothes. I got a gun here I'll trade you for them."

He said, "Hunnicutt's gun, I'll bet. What'd you do, shoot the old son-of-a-bitch?"

I shook my head as I handed down the gun. "I didn't shoot nobody."

He was checking the loads in the gun, and smelling the barrel. He said, "You didn't shoot him with this gun anyways. Now let me have the whole of it."

I said, "I can't do that. You going to give me some clothes for that gun or ain't you?" I was scared and edgy and my voice was what you'd call feisty, I guess.

I ain't never seen a man move no faster than this one did. One minute he was standing there with his rifle under his arm and that pistol in his hand. The next he'd leaped at me, grabbed my leg and yanked me out of the saddle like I wasn't nothing at all. I hit the ground on my back and it knocked the wind out of me. I gasped and choked, trying to fill my lungs. He waited until I had, then he kicked me hard in the belly. He said, "You little bastard, come clean with me or I'll kick you 'til you can't even crawl, let alone walk or ride a horse!"

I looked up at those cold eyes and that slit of a mouth and I knew he'd do exactly what he said he would. It was like I was back home again, with Pa standing over me with a razor strop. I nodded. "I'll tell you. Can I sit up?"

He nodded. I've never been much of a liar and I knew any lie I told would be spotted by this man right away. So I figured I'd better tell the truth. I had a hunch them cattle down in the corral was Hunnicutt cattle and that this man had no love for the Hunnicutt outfit, from the way he'd talked.

I said, "I was workin' for Mr. Hunnicutt. Doin' chores. I only been there about a week."

He said impatiently, "Come on. Come on. I ain't got all day." He looked back in the direction I had come as he spoke, nervously.

I said, "Last night I got up to go to the outhouse. That's how come I ain't got nothin' on but my underwear. I was goin' back in the bunkhouse when Mr. Hunnicutt rides up to the kitchen door an' goes inside. He goes upstairs, and I hear yellin' an' screamin', an' pretty soon the light comes downstairs agin an' I hear a shot. I went to the window an' looked in an' there's Mr. Hunnicutt on the floor with blood all over him, an' Mr. Donahue in his underwear holdin' a gun an' Mrs. Hunnicutt in her nightgown lookin' on. I was scared an' backed away but I fell over a pail somebody'd left there an' they heard me an' come runnin' out. I knew they'd say I done it, so I jumped on Mr. Hunnicutt's horse an' took out of there. I was a good piece away from there before they commenced yellin' an' screechin' an' shootin'. I figure they're sayin' I done it an' I figure if they catch me, they'll sure railroad me to jail—or string me up."

He went over to Mr. Hunnicutt's horse and took down the saddlebags. He went through what was in them after dumping them out on the ground. He found the paper and picked it up. He read it, frowning and slow, and I guessed he wasn't much better a reader than me. He looked at me. "You know what this is?"

"Yes sir."

"Hunnicutt write it?"

"He must of. It was in his saddlebags."

A strange kind of gleam had come into the man's cold eyes. He said, "Get up an' come in the shack. I got some clothes you can wear. Then we got to get rid of Hunnicutt's horse, an' the tracks he made comin' here."

I didn't know how he was going to do that, or why, and I knew I neither liked nor trusted him. But there wasn't nothing else. There wasn't no other choice.

He picked up the things he'd dumped out of the saddlebags and put them back. He put the paper in his pocket after carefully folding it.

CHAPTER 4

The man rummaged around in an old trunk inside the shack and finally tossed me a pair of pants, a shirt and boots, all of which was too big for me. He found an old, crumpled hat that was also too big but I took it anyway. While I dressed, he said, "Name's Hank Sligh. Them cattle in the corral is wearin' a Hunnicutt brand, in case you're wonderin'. Now that you've made a trail here, I don't dare keep 'em or even drive 'em where I was meanin' to. So you can see you cost me plenty, you little son-of-a-bitch!"

I didn't like him and I didn't like the way he talked to me, but I wasn't in no position to protest. He wouldn't let me leave, even if I wanted to. When I'd finished dressing, he said sourly, "Come on. Hurry up."

We went outside. He got hisself a horse out of the corral, saddled him, then mounted and opened the corral gate. He yelled at me, "Get mounted. I'm goin' to let a bunch of these cattle out. I want you to drive 'em back along the trail you made comin' here. You think you can do that without wanderin' off the trail?"

I said, "I can do it."

He cut the bunch of cattle in the corral about in two and drove the first half out. I drove them back along the trail I'd made coming here. I could see the tracks of my horse plain enough, even where the grass was high because there was a path in it where it had been crushed by my horse's hoofs. I looked back and saw Sligh bringing the other half of the bunch, using them to obliterate the trail Mr. Hunnicutt's horse had made behind the first bunch.

It was clever, but by now I had realized that Sligh was a rustler. Cleverness and rustling just naturally go together. Sligh was a good name for him. He was sly and hard and cruel and I had the feeling he'd kill me just as quick as look at me if it suited his purposes.

It didn't suit his purposes now. The will Mr. Hunnicutt had scrawled out on a piece of paper had stirred the greed in him. He was wondering how he was going to use it and thinking that maybe, by using it and me, he could get his greedy hands on the Hunnicutt ranch.

So for now, at least, I was safe. Sligh wouldn't hurt me because he needed me. He wasn't going to let either the Hunnicutt hands or a posse from town get hold of me if it could be helped.

I drove the cattle along at a steady pace for about five miles. Since I'd come from Hunnicutt's, the direction I drove them was back toward it. Later, after Mr. Hunnicutt's horse had been trailed here Sligh could say that the cattle wandered into his yard at dusk. He'd say he had corralled them overnight and started them back toward Hunnicutt's the next morning. Donahue might know he was lying but he wouldn't be able to prove anything.

Sligh finally left the bunch he was driving and rode to me. He put his horse right up beside mine and said, "Get on behind me. But first tie your horse's reins together and hook them over the saddle horn.

I did as I was told. With the reins tied up, the horse wouldn't be able to lower his head enough to graze. He'd head back toward Hunnicutt's in a straight line without wandering and dawdling the way a horse would that was able to graze as he went.

Sligh went back and drove the bunch that had been behind me in with the others. He continued driving them for another two or three miles.

Hunnicutt's horse just stood there as if wondering what to do. I thought maybe he'd try following us, but he didn't. After a few tries at grazing, he headed back toward Hunnicutt's.

Sligh was taking a big chance, driving these cattle, hiding me, being seen with Mr. Hunnicutt's horse in broad daylight. But he probably knew that it would be a while before those trailing me caught up. He knew I'd traveled most of the previous night and that nobody could have trailed me successfully in the dark.

Sligh left the cattle a full ten miles from his shack. Then he headed west for several miles before heading home again. He didn't want his horse's tracks anywhere near those of Mr. Hunnicutt's.

Going back, he headed his horse toward the foot of a rocky bluff. At the bottom of the slope leading up to it he stopped. He pointed at a hole in the bluff, a kind of natural cave. "See that?"

"Yes, sir."

"Hop off onto this big rock just beside the horse. Work your way up to that cave without touching ground. There's plenty of rocks on the slope for you to do that."

I said, "Yes, sir."

"Stay there. I'll bring you some food and water, but not until that bunch that's chasing you has come and gone."

I jumped off his horse onto the big rock. He rode on, and

I made my way up the slope, stepping from rock to rock so as to leave no trail.

The cave was about eight feet deep. When I got clear to the back, it was dry and warm and I couldn't see the foot of the slope. It was kind of dark and I figured nobody could see me even if they were looking straight into the cave. Not unless I had a fire and I wasn't stupid enough for that. Besides, I didn't have any matches.

I wondered how long it was going to be before Sligh brought me water and food. I considered leaving and trying to get away by myself but I gave up the idea almost at once. Afoot, I couldn't travel more than ten or fifteen miles a day to save my life. Sligh could cover fifty or more on a horse. He'd catch me and I knew instinctively that when he did he'd beat me worse than Pa ever had.

So all I could do was wait. And think.

Sligh meant to hide me from the Hunnicutt crew and from any posses that came after me. But only because of that will. Except for that, he'd have turned me over to them. Now that the Hunnicutt cattle were gone from his corral he didn't have to worry about any accusations of rustling I might make. He wasn't in possession of any stolen cattle, and nobody could prove he had ever been.

But what good would the will be to him? Even if it was proper, and even if it was recognized by the courts, I couldn't inherit nothing while a murder charge hung over me. Maybe Sligh would try to clear me, I thought, by naming Donahue. I shook my head. Sligh's word would have no weight. No more than would mine. I finally decided he was just hoping. There wasn't no risk involved for him and if he did figure something out the rewards could be pretty big.

Thinking it over, I didn't like the fix I was in now any better than I'd liked being alone on the Wyoming prairie without a horse or food. I'd run away from home to keep from gettin' beat, but I had a feeling in my bones that Sligh would beat me first time I crossed him, and worse than Pa ever had.

Besides that, I was in his power as completely as if I'd been a black slave that he owned, body and soul. All he had to do was turn me over to the law, or to Hunnicutt hands. I had the notion that Mr. Hunnicutt had been pretty well liked, both by his neighbors and the men who worked for him.

I went to the mouth of the cave and stared out across the prairie. I could see a little band of antelope about half a mile away. Otherwise there wasn't nothing.

I went back in the cave and laid down. I tried to sleep, knowing that would help to pass the time. I was hungry by now, and thirsty, but I knew it might be tomorrow before Sligh brought me anything.

I finally slept, and I waked to hear a shout. I ran to the mouth of the cave, thinking it was Sligh, but it wasn't. There was a bunch of maybe twenty or twenty-five men riding along at the foot of the bluff. I recognized Donahue, and Ike the blacksmith, and a couple of other Hunnicutt hands. They was trailing Sligh's horse, having been as confused by his ruse as he had known they'd be. They knew I'd been riding Hunnicutt's horse, but he'd been riderless when they caught up with him. They'd probably back-tracked, to where the cattle trail and that of Hunnicutt's horse come together. After that, they'd trailed the cattle back to Sligh's and, getting no satisfaction from him, had returned and followed his trail on the chance that he'd helped me get away and had hidden me. I don't suppose I was heavy enough for them to notice the difference in the weight Sligh's horse had been carrying. After going without food so long, and traveling so hard, I doubted if I weighed more than a sack of grain.

They didn't stop at the foot of the bluff, but kept going, talking back and forth between themselves. I kept myself out of sight until they was a quarter mile away.

It was late afternoon by now and Sligh would be coming with food and water for me before nightfall, or shortly afterwards. I knowed I couldn't just sit here and let him use me, make a slave out of me like I was an animal. Maybe he'd catch me and maybe he'd beat me half to death, but if I didn't try now I wasn't going to get another chance.

The Hunnicutt crew was now more than half a mile away. They turned around the end of the bluff and disappeared.

Walking on rocks, I headed along the slope, not going straight downhill the way I'd come up, but angling. I was careful and I took my time and I didn't make no tracks. I got to the foot of the bluff and stopped, trying to decide which way to go. South, I decided. North was Sioux country and dangerous.

I sat down on a rock and took off the boots Sligh had given me. My own feet were horny and callused from going barefoot most of the time back home, so it wasn't going to bother me. Carrying the boots and nothing else, I picked my way southward, praying silently that I could get a couple of miles away before Sligh showed up. Or better still, stay away from him until it got dark.

A feeling of having to hurry bothered me and I kept looking back, but at the same time I knew that hurry wouldn't help me if I left so much as a single track. Sometimes I stepped carefully on clumps of curly buffalo grass, sliding my toes into the clump carefully each time so that I wouldn't bend or break any of the dry stems sticking up for eight inches or so. Sometimes I stepped on rocks. Where I had no choice but to put my foot down on bare ground, I turned, and knelt and brushed the track out carefully. He might be able to trail me and he might find me in the end, but I was going to make trailing me so slow that he'd either give up or I'd have a chance to get away.

It was tiring, and the sun was setting when I finally stopped, sat on a rock and stared back at the cave up in the rocky bluff. It looked like a black dot but I realized that I had only covered a little more than a mile.

I hoped Sligh would wait until dark to come. I had an idea he would suspect Red Donahue of leaving a couple of men someplace nearby to keep an eye on him.

After dark, I would no longer be able to hide my trail. I'd have to go on, making as much haste as I could throughout the night. At daybreak, I could try hiding my trail again.

I traveled steadily until it was too dark to see the ground. I was ravenously hungry and my mouth felt like it was full of cotton. I hadn't crossed a trickle of water, but suddenly I heard the sound of water ahead of me. I broke into a run, falling down twice before I reached it. It wasn't more than two feet wide and the water was strong with alkali, but it was the sweetest water I ever drank. I drank as much as I dared. I soaked my feet in it and splashed water into my face and wet my hair with it.

I'd heard you could hide your trail by traveling in water and I knew I'd been angling steadily west. So, walking in the narrow stream, barefooted, I headed east. Sligh would waste several hours following the little stream west before he turned around and rode back the other way.

I stayed in the stream for more than an hour. When I left it, it was where the grass was short and thick and where my tracks would be hard to find after twelve hours or so had passed.

I was pretty tired now but I didn't stop. When your life depends on keeping going, you can stand a lot of tiredness. And my life did depend on it.

At dawn, I spooked a rabbit out of a clump of sagebrush. I snatched up a rock and ran after him and when he ducked into another bush, I threw the rock and hit him with enough force to stun him. I dragged him out, killed him with a chop of my hand on the back of his neck. I literally tore the hide off him and the guts out of him. I wished I had some matches but I didn't, so I ate as much of the rabbit as I could raw. Then, taking my boots off again and carrying what was left of the rabbit in the other hand, I went straight south, again stepping from grass clump to grass clump and from rock to rock.

I didn't bother to look behind no more. If Sligh caught up with me it wasn't going to help me any to know that he was coming.

But I did watch ahead and to both sides, ready to take cover the minute anyone appeared.

CHAPTER 5

I knew the Indians had seen me a long time before I saw them because when I finally did see them, they was heading straight toward me, not hurrying as if they was thirsty for my blood, but slowly and cautiously as if they wondered what the hell I was doing out here all alone. I suppose to anyone watching I was behaving in a mighty peculiar manner, a partly consumed raw rabbit in one hand, boots in the other, dressed in clothes that fit like gunnysacks.

There was six of them and I couldn't have told what tribe they belonged to, but hereabouts was the country of the Cheyennes, or at least it had been before the white men grabbed it away from them.

I knew it wasn't no good to run, and I didn't have nothing to fight with. Before they reached me, I put the rabbit carcass down on a rock and sat down and pulled on my boots. Then I stood up and faced them, knowing they'd probably kill me, or maybe torture me and that there wasn't one damn' thing I could do to stop them. There was rocks lying around, though, and I made up my mind that before they took me I'd put up the best kind of fight I could. Truth was, I was beginning to get a little mad. It seemed to me like everybody I ran into used me and I was getting sick of it.

These Indians didn't wear feathered headdresses the way Indians did in the pictures I had seen. They'd have one, or maybe two feathers sticking out of their hair, but two of them didn't have no feathers at all. They all wore their hair in braids, lying one on each side and down their naked chests, and they wore leather pants that was pretty greasy but decorated with what I supposed was colored thread. I later learned they was porcupine quills. Two of them had rifles, the old single-shot kind, and the others had bows and quivers slung over their backs with maybe six or eight arrows in each.

Indians must like spotted ponies, because four of their horses was spotted, three brown and white, one black and white. The other two horses was grays.

They didn't say a word but just rode up to within about fifty feet of me and stopped. They kept looking past me, like I was pulling some kind of trick.

I'd never wanted to see Sligh again, but now I found myself wishing he'd come into sight trailing me. Suddenly the Indians began to talk to each other, in their own language which was just so much gibberish to me. Two of them slid off their ponies and ran at me. It was so quick I was almost taken by surprise, but I had time to stoop and grab up a rock I'd spotted. One of them hit me and knocked me down, but I slammed the rock against his head and he didn't move after he hit the ground. The other one was on top of me, and I tried to hit him with the rock too but he was a lot bigger than me and he twisted it out of my hand. I tried to bite him, and he cuffed me on the side of the head hard enough to make my ears ring before he yanked me to my feet. The one I'd hit still lay without moving on the ground.

The oldest of the bunch, who was about the same age as Pa, was scowling, but gradually the scowl disappeared. It was like he'd been irritated at first to see one of his friends knocked cold, but once he'd had time to think on it, he kind of admired me for fighting back against such topheavy odds.

The one Indian was still holding me and the one I'd hit was beginning to groan and stir. Pretty soon he opened his eyes and sat up, scowling at me as if he'd like to slit my throat with the knife he carried in a leather scabbard at his belt. The old one said something to him and he staggered to his horse. The one who held me dragged me over to his horse and boosted me up. Then he leaped up behind me and the whole outfit kicked their ponies in the ribs and galloped away in the direction they had come.

I was scared. I don't mind admitting it. I'd heard about what Indians do to the whites they capture. I'd probably be screaming the first few minutes after they started on me, but I gritted my teeth and made up my mind I was going to take as much as I could. A man only dies once; he ought to do it right if he can.

One thing, I thought as we rode away, me bouncing up and down and only the Indian behind me keeping me on the horse. Sligh wasn't going to get his hands on me. He might trail me, but when he found where the Indians had captured me, he'd give up.

Or would he? Except for Mr. Hunnicutt's will, I knew he would. But he had ideas about getting his hands on the Hunnicutt ranch, all of its hundreds of thousands of acres and all of its thousands of cattle. He needed me for that so maybe he *would* come after me.

I began to hope he would. A beating at Sligh's hands

would sure beat getting tortured to death by these savages.

We rode almost straight south for several hours. I wondered what the Indians had been doing up here, but I didn't spend much time worrying about it. Indians wandered all over, I had heard. They hunted and they stole horses, both from the whites and from each other. Since the buffalo had mostly disappeared, they probably killed cattle when they figured they could get away with it.

Toward nightfall, we came to a little stream with willows and cottonwoods growing along its bank and entered an Indian village. It wasn't very big. I counted twenty-five tepees. A lot of dogs came out and barked at us, probably because they caught my strange smell. The Indian riding behind me shoved me off the horse. I stumbled and fell, but I got right up again.

The old one pushed me toward one of the tepees after giving his horse to a boy about my age. I went in through the flap. It smelled smoky inside, but there was a fire going in the middle, with the smoke rising to the peak where a hole let it get out. There was a woman squatting beside the fire stirring something in a pot. The Indian said something to her and she brought me a dish of meat and gravy. The dish seemed to have been carved of wood, but it was so soaked with grease that it was hard to tell. I was starved but I couldn't eat until I had something to drink. I made a sign of drinking and the man gave me a skin water bag. I drank and then started in on the food. I began to feel a little hope because I didn't figure they'd feed me if they were going to kill me afterward. Besides, so far nobody had hurt me and maybe they wasn't going to.

The Indian went out, leaving me alone in the tepee with

the squaw. It was hard to tell what her thoughts was because her face and eyes was so expressionless.

I finished eating and the squaw gave me some more, and I ate that too. I'd heard that Indian squaws don't have much to say about what their men do, so I guessed I'd risk it and just get up and leave. I bowed, and smiled, and thanked the woman for the food in English. I knew she couldn't understand my words, but I thought she understood what I meant because a little bit of a smile showed on her face. I stepped outside.

The sun was down and it was gray with dusk. Some Indian children was playing nearby and Indian grown-ups moved around without paying much attention to me. That kind of puzzled me. If I'd been important enough to capture and bring here by force, why wasn't I important enough to guard?

The answer to that was obvious. They hadn't captured me. They didn't intend either to kill or torture me. That sudden realization made me feel so weak that I had to sit down. I sat on the ground in front of the tepee. Hell, Indians wasn't savage monsters. They was just people like everybody else, even if they did live in hide tepees instead of houses and even if they didn't farm the way white men did.

They'd found me wandering around alone in a thousand square miles of empty prairie and they'd figured I needed help. Which I sure did, even if I wouldn't have admitted it.

I decided to test my new idea. I got up and walked down the street between the tepees to the stream. A woman was getting water, and out in the middle a man was taking a bath. I walked down the stream for a couple of hundred yards. Nobody paid any attention to me and nobody came after me.

Well, as soon as I found out I could leave if I wanted to, I didn't specially want to leave. I was dead tired for one thing, and I hadn't been eating too regular. As long as they didn't intend to kill or torture me, it wouldn't hurt nothing to stay for a day or two. I wasn't going to get far on foot and maybe later I could steal one of their horses and get clear away from this damned empty windy country and from the men who seemed determined to use me as a goat for what they'd done themselves.

The thought of stealing a horse from people who had befriended me made me feel guilty, but I fought down the guilt. All I wanted to do was survive. People had been using me and for once it wouldn't hurt if I used somebody else.

It was dark now, so I went back to the tepee where I'd been fed. I'd of knocked before going in but there wasn't nothing to knock on. So I pushed aside the flap and went inside.

The man was there now, along with the squaw. He said something to me and pointed to a pile of buffalo robes on one side of the tepee. I figured this was where he wanted me to sleep, so I went over there, laid down and covered up. I went to sleep almost right away.

It was light when I woke up. I got up and went out. It seemed like everyone was down at the stream, either getting water in water skins or washing, or taking a bath. There was some women out in the stream, naked, and there was some men, but they didn't seem to be paying any attention to each other. I splashed some water in my face, and washed my hands with sand and water.

There was a ridge behind the camp. I climbed it and from its top I could see the Indian pony herd, grazing on the other side of the stream and beyond a little rise. Several Indian boys was standing guard.

It wasn't going to be easy stealing a horse. I figured the herd was guarded all the time, maybe to keep the horses from wandering too far away, maybe to give the alarm in case Indians from another tribe came on a horse stealing raid.

I walked back to the village. The squaw gave me some food that I gulped like I hadn't eaten for a week. She gave me some more and I gulped that too. I was so thin I guess I wouldn't have weighed a hundred pounds soaking wet, but then I'd always been kind of thin. Back home there hadn't been much food, and when there was plenty it was mostly root vegetables and greens in the summertime. Damn' little meat, and what we had was mostly fat.

Well, back home Ma and Pa worked like slaves from dawn to dusk. This was some different. The Indian men sat in front of the tepees, smoking and talking. One was making arrows, and another was chipping away at a stone, making a tomahawk. Inside the tepees the squaws was working on leather pants or shirts or moccasins. A few was working outside on stiff buffalo hides, softening them so they could be used, taking the hair off after it had been loosened by something they spread on the hides. The children played, and yelled and seemed to be having a good time. It put me in mind of the fact that I'd been working ever since I was big enough and had never played, or had anybody to play with, or even known how to play.

Everybody says Indians are stupid savages, but these people didn't look neither stupid or savage to me. They looked like they was living a damn' good life, doing what was needed to stay alive, but enjoying it along the way. All the time I was in that Indian village I never saw an adult strike a child.

Still, I couldn't stay. Sooner or later, Sligh was going to unravel my trail. He'd find where the Indians had taken me. He'd follow the trail of the Indians' horses without any trouble at all.

So I had to get away and to do that I had to steal me a horse, whether I liked doing it or not. So I watched and waited. The guards on the horse herd was boys about my age or younger. I'd have to take a horse around dusk in the evening. They couldn't follow me in the dark and I'd have a chance to get away.

That evening, around sundown, I waded across the stream and climbed the little rise behind where the pony herd was. I stopped short of the top and looked over.

The horses was about the same distance from me as the boys who was guarding them. It was now or never. I got up and sprinted for the horses. Only I hadn't counted on the fact that I'd scare them and not be able to catch one right away. The horses spooked away and the boys reached me and knocked me to the ground. I got up, ready to fight, but it wasn't no use. They was on me and they held my arms and dragged me back to the village, to the tepee where I'd slept the night before.

The old Indian talked to me sternly in his own tongue, which I didn't understand, but I knew what he was saying. The boys left and I ate and went to bed, wishing I could tell the man that Sligh was coming, and maybe Donahue and the Hunnicutt crew too, and maybe even a posse from the town nearest to the ranch.

But I couldn't talk Cheyenne and none of them spoke English. It looked like I couldn't get away and if I stayed there was sure to be trouble coming for these Indians.

One thing. I was getting tired of having everything decided for me. I'd run away from home so I could have some say in what happened to me. Before I was through, I was going to have that say, no matter who got hurt along the way.

CHAPTER 6

I woke up pretty early, before the sky was light, worrying. I kept trying to figure out how I could tell the old Indian what was coming. I finally decided I'd try by drawing a picture for him on the ground.

I got up and washed, and as soon as the old Indian came out of the tepee rubbing his eyes, I picked up a stick and began drawing on the ground. I beckoned him to come and look and he was curious enough to come.

I drew a stick figure and then pointed to myself. I made the figure running and then behind it I drew fifteen or twenty others, riding horses and also running, pursuing me. I used the stick as a make-believe rifle and pointed it at him and said "bang," and then I pointed it at the other lodges and said "bang" each time.

Well, he understood all right. He motioned me to come inside and once in there, told his wife to feed me, and to get together a sack of food for me. He went outside and shouted for someone to get a horse for me. I couldn't understand his words, of course, but I understood the urgency in him well enough.

I gulped the food, a little excited at the thought of getting away again. When I had finished, I took the food that the woman had put into a beaded pouch and went outside.

I looked north and I knew right away that it was too late. They raised a column of dust that must have been a hundred feet high, so I guessed there were a lot of them. The boy still hadn't brought the horse and there wasn't a horse in camp at this time of day.

The old Indian shouted and another Indian who must have been around thirty came and beckoned me. Right away it looked like they intended to hide me and not turn me over to the men chasing me. I had a hunch that was a mistake but I was grateful for it.

I followed the Indian and he went into a dry gulch that fed down into the stream bed where the village was. The horsemen were still more than a mile away so I knew they couldn't have seen me yet.

The gulch narrowed as we traveled and its sides grew steeper. We traveled for what seemed like a mile and finally the gulch leveled out where it began to climb up a mountainside. From here we could see the village plain as could be. The horsemen was just at the edge of it, walking their horses now. I recognized Donahue at their head in spite of the distance. I thought the man beside him was Sligh, but I couldn't tell for sure. Counting, I made out thirty-two men in the group, too many for the Indians to fight even if they'd been a mind.

Several Indian men came out, wearing their ceremonial headdresses. Two were feathered, with feathers going 'way down their backs. The other was a buffalo scalp with the horns attached. They had what looked like pipes in their hands.

The two groups talked for a long, long time. The horses of the white men began to fidget and dance around from being held still after traveling hard so long. It was too far away to see signs, but plainly the Indians were saying I wasn't in their camp. The whites were as insistent that I was, probably saying they'd tracked me to where the Indians picked me up and then had tracked the Indians here.

It looked like a Mexican standoff, only it wasn't because the whites had the upper hand. Finally half a dozen of the whites got off their horses and began to make a search of the tepees.

The Indian with me muttered something. I looked at him and saw that his face was flushed, his eyes narrowed with anger.

And then, so suddenly I couldn't have said what caused it, all hell broke loose down there. Maybe an Indian fired first. Maybe there was a scuffle and a white man fired first. But the reports came crackling and the puffs of powdersmoke and there was Indians running back and forth in the village like ants when you disturb their anthill. The whites galloped back to the edge of the village, leaving one of their number on the ground, motionless, and leaving two horses crippled and hobbling first one way and then the other, not knowing which way to go to get away.

The man with me got up and started for the village. He turned his head and looked back at me. His face was white now with fury and shock and his eyes was the coldest, cruelest eyes I've ever seen, excepting Sligh. He raised his gun and pointed it at me and I knew he was going to kill me unless something stopped him and it sure didn't look like anything would. I reckoned the time for dying was here right now and I felt like begging, only I knew it wouldn't do no good. I stood up, trying not to let him see how scared I was. I looked him straight in the eye. I'd faced death once before just before Mr. Hunnicutt found me and saved my life and I'd had myself all screwed up to die like a man ought to die. Now I screwed myself up again. My knees and hands was shaking so bad I didn't know how he could help but see, but by God, I looked him straight in the eye and I didn't let my stare waver a bit. Where he'd shoot me I didn't know but I hoped it would be where it'd be quick and over with right away. Dying is bad enough, without spending hours in agony waiting for it to come.

It was real strange. Them cold, cruel eyes began to get less cold and cruel and finally he lowered the gun. He wasn't no less furious and his face was still white and tight, but he wasn't mad at me no more. He kind of gave me a short nod and then he turned and ran back down the gulch toward the sound of firing. He didn't have to tell me to stay hidden because I knew what would happen to me if I was found.

Well, coming that close to death and suddenly being spared makes a man's knees turn to water and makes his chest feel like there ain't nothing in it any more. I sat down hard and began to shake and I guess I sat there shaking for more than ten minutes before it stopped. All this time Donahue and Sligh and the others were riding back and forth in the Indian village, shooting everything that moved, even the dogs. Some of the Indians escaped, going up the creek and up into ravines like the one I was in, but most of them got slaughtered there in the village. It was so early in the morning that most of them had been in bed, and some asleep, and they hadn't had time to more than snatch up their weapons, mostly bows and arrows, and run outside into that hail of lead.

It made me sick at my stomach and the food the squaw had given me was like a lump of lead in my gut. I hadn't been here long, but I'd begun to like the Indians and I sure admired the way they lived, doing what was needed and getting along with each other and not bothering anyone. There was no way I was responsible for what had happened. The Indians had taken me against my will and had prevented me from getting away. I had no control over Donahue and Sligh and the other whites. But I couldn't help thinking that if it wasn't for me, none of it would ever have happened at all.

Once all resistance in the Indian village stopped, Donahue and Sligh and those with them milled around for a while as if they didn't know what to do. They went into the tepees and came out with their arms loaded with loot, I supposed beaded moccasins and buffalo robes, and pipe pouches and whatever else took their fancy. They stepped over the dead Indians as if they wasn't human at all, but only dead animals, like wolves or coyotes, and a lot of them dead Indians was little kids, some no more than a couple of years old and barely able to walk.

I felt myself getting madder all the time. I wished I was fifty men and could go down there and take revenge for the murdered Indians. I wished I could leave them white men scattered around dead like the Indians was. The Indians might of captured me, but I had a feeling they'd rescued me more than they'd captured me. The same way Mr. Hunnicutt had when he'd found me wandering around all alone.

I remembered wondering how it could be, when people was sent to prison all the time for stealing things like food, that men was able to get away with murder like this without any penalty. It didn't seem right and I knew it wasn't right, but I guess even then I knew it was part of an imperfect world and had to be accepted along with all the world's other imperfections, unless you was able to do something about it, which I wasn't. Not now at least.

But I was adding up a score, as clearly in my mind as if it was written down. Sometime that score was going to be settled. Maybe the law couldn't touch these men for what they had done, but one way or another they had to pay.

As soon as they'd got everything they wanted out of the Indian lodges, they roped the tepee poles at the tops and pulled the lodges down. Being there was fires in all of them, it wasn't long before smoke began to raise up in the air. Buffalo hide lodges don't burn too easily, but when they do catch, they burn fiercely, sending great plumes of oily smoke up into the air. Indians had survived the killing, but when they went back to where their village had been, they'd find their food and shelter and everything they owned either stolen or destroyed.

Well, I didn't have too much time to think about that. Down the gulch toward the village, I heard the straining, toiling sounds of some Indians coming toward me. I suppose I should have guessed some would come up the gulch I was in, but I hadn't, and now it was too late to get away. If I ran across that empty hillside, the white men down below were sure to see me. If I stayed, there was a good chance the escaping Indians would kill me in revenge for what the whites had done to them. I couldn't honestly blame them, neither. In their place, I'd of done the same.

So for the third time I now faced death and having done it twice before, I found I was able to do it with more dignity even though the same cold ball of fear was in my gut. I stood up, and faced toward them, and I folded my arms and waited for whatever they decided to do with me.

It was a small party, one man, middle-aged, two women, one old and one young, and three children, the oldest of which was probably eleven, the youngest barely able to walk.

The man had a tomahawk, and the young woman had a knife. They stopped when they saw me, their faces showing first surprise and then anger, hatred and the purposefulness that told me I'd either have to run, fight, or die.

I didn't move. Arms folded, I stared calmly at them. At least I tried to make my face look calm. It had worked before, with the Indian who had brought me here. It just might work again.

The women and children stayed back and the man advanced warily. I didn't say anything, because I knew I wouldn't be understood. The man came to within ten feet of me and stopped.

He frowned as if he didn't know what to do. The older squaw screeched something at him and he turned to look at her. He half-raised the tomahawk, which was made out of stone bound to a heavy stick with rawhide. He took a step toward me. Suddenly he stopped. He turned his head and spoke to the old squaw. He beckoned the bunch of them and they walked past me about twenty feet away, heading for higher ground. They were visible to the white men down below, but I doubted if they'd be pursued. They disappeared over the crest of a shallow rise and I turned back toward the burning village down below.

I knew one thing for sure. Donahue couldn't afford to come this far without making a thorough search for me. He had to *know* that I was dead. If possible he had to have my body to take back with him.

They'd searched the lodges at the same time they'd

looted them. Now they moved among the dead Indians, looking at each one to make sure I wasn't one of them.

Soon they'd come scouring the surrounding area. They *knew* that I'd been in the Indian village. They had read trail to where I had been picked up.

They knew I was either around nearby or that I'd escaped. If the first was true, they'd find me if they had to turn over every rock for a mile around. If I'd escaped, they'd find my trail and follow it.

But there was one thing they wasn't counting on. They thought I was still wearing the clothes I'd been wearing when I left Sligh's place, including the boots that didn't fit. They'd be looking for a trail left by those boots. They wouldn't be expecting me to be wearing Indian clothes.

A dozen or more trails led away from the murdered village down below. Mine would be one of them, indistinguishable from the others.

So all I had to do was find a place to hide, a hole I could crawl into so that they couldn't find me when they searched.

But where, on this rolling, empty plain could I find such a place? The grass was high, so I got down and crawled through it, following the general direction that the Indians had gone. There just plain wasn't no holes. There wasn't no place to hide and I was going to get caught.

But damn it, I wasn't going to stop fighting until I was. I wasn't going to give up.

Once over the rise, I began to run. It was panic that made me run, but I couldn't seem to keep it down. Running, I fell into another dry wash, heading away from the village instead of toward it.

It gave me momentary cover at least. Scrambling, running, sometimes falling, I traveled down that high-walled gully getting more panicky all the time. Finally, sweating, hot, out of breath and close to exhaustion, I stopped. I sat down and I prayed. I had no faith that praying would do no good, but it was the only thing that I had left.

CHAPTER 7

I could hear the shouts of the searchers echoing back and forth. They was planning now, having decided that a haphazard search wasn't going to do them no good. I crawled to the lip of the wash and looked over.

They had formed a line, like the spoke of a wheel, and while the man who formed the hub stayed on the outskirts of the burning village, the line of mounted men rotated around him, sweeping an area that must have been a quarter of a mile in diameter. I was more than half a mile away, so they didn't come close enough to worry me.

On the next sweep, the pivot man followed the tracks of the man who had been farthest out on the first sweep and I could see that this time the man farthest out would come within a few hundred yards of me.

I slipped back down into the wash and ran along its bottom. Their search was thorough, and they'd find me eventually, since on each sweep the horsemen was no more than fifty feet apart. There was only two ways I could escape. One was to creep back down the wash while the searchers was on the far side of the village and hide somewhere in the burning village itself. The other was to find a place to hide.

Going back down the wash was risky, because I knew Sligh and Donahue was smart and would consider the possibility I might do just that. They'd have stationed a man in each of the dry gulches which was deep enough to conceal me as I returned.

I gave that idea up right away, and that left me with the choice either of finding a place to hide or giving myself up.

Damned if I was going to give myself up, I kept going, and suddenly I saw something I thought might do.

A tree grew right at the lip of the wash, which here was maybe four feet deep. Flood water from cloudbursts had undercut its roots, leaving them exposed. Undercut that way, the tree had leaned toward the wash, the other half of its roots keeping it from toppling in. I tried crawling under the roots, but saw right away that the cavity wasn't big enough. Besides that, my tracks led straight to the root cavity under the twisted tree.

Beginning to feel a little panicky, I began to dig with my hands. I threw the dry dirt down to cover my tracks, scattering it so that it wouldn't be too noticeable. There was other moccasin tracks going up the wash so I knowed if I hid mine where they climbed the side of the wash, the searchers probably wouldn't notice nothing out of the way.

Hiding myself was something else. I dug like a badger, as fast as I could. Here, under the tree's roots, it was hot and airless and in minutes I was soaked with sweat. I realized, too, that if I undercut the tree too much, it would topple further, imprisoning me in its root cage so that I'd not be able to get away.

Still, when you're faced with certain death on one hand and possible death on the other, it ain't hard to choose.

I heard someone coming up the wash and froze, scrooching back as far as I could. A squaw with a little boy maybe two years old hurried up the bottom of the gulch. She saw me, and gazed curiously for a moment. Then she went on, making no sound, saying nothing. I wondered if she'd be all right, or if they'd kill her just for the sport of it. The little boy didn't see me at all.

As soon as they passed from sight, I commenced digging again. The dirt I took out was soft, almost sandy, and I used it to build a wall between myself and the gulch itself. Hearing a shout, I stopped digging and froze again, hardly daring to breathe.

Peering through the network of roots, I saw the legs of a horse as his rider came along the lip of the wash. The tree shifted and sifted dirt down on me as another rider skirted its base. One of the men, the one whose horse I couldn't see said, "Ike, is he under them roots? That's a good place to hide."

I heard the blacksmith's voice answering, "Naw. There ain't a big enough hole under there to hide a cottontail."

I was shaking like a cottontail. I saw a little stream of earth run to the bottom of the wash, but by then the two horsemen had gone by. I could hear their voices going away.

Ike had seen me. He couldn't of helped doing so. I'd been able to see the legs of his horse and while maybe he hadn't seen my face, he must of seen my legs. I thought, thank God it was Ike on the far side of the gully and not the other man. And I decided that maybe there was a God after all and that maybe He was looking after me. Out of thirty men, it had been Ike who had spotted me, the only man of the thirty who wouldn't give me away. Ike knew I hadn't killed Mr. Hunnicutt. He knew about Donahue and Mrs. Hunnicutt. He was around the ranch yard all the time and there probably wasn't much he didn't see.

One thing I knew as I crouched there, sweating and trembling, I'd never hunt rabbits again. Once you know how it feels to be hunted, you lose interest in hunting other living things.

I could still hear them shouting. Once I heard a volley of shots and supposed they'd caught up with one of the Indians. Maybe a wounded brave who had the gall to shoot at them, I thought. Or maybe only the squaw with the little boy. I was learning something else. People out here mostly didn't consider Indians human at all. Killing them wasn't murder no more than killing a coyote was.

I'd brought all this trouble to the Indians. It was because of me that they'd been attacked, their village burned and a good many of them killed. If it hadn't been for the fact that I hadn't had anything to say about being in their village the guilt would have been unbearable.

It was silent at last as the shadows cast by the rays of the sun lengthened. Careful and suspicious, I crawled out from beneath the tree. It creaked, and settled several inches farther toward the gulch. I got out quickly then, and watched it slip a little more.

I crawled to the lip of the wash, sticking only enough of my head over the top to see. I stayed there like that for a long time, looking at the nearby hills. Finally I saw something move at the crest of one, and watching another, saw something move up there too.

They were watching. They knew that I was here. They hadn't been able to find me, but they figured if they pretended to leave, I'd come out and they could capture me.

I slid back down into the wash. I was hungry and thirsty

by now, but I could wait. They'd give up at dark, and I could wait that long. Maybe they'd figure they had killed me along with the Indians in the village and hadn't recognized me because I'd have been dressed in Indian clothes.

The sun sank behind the horizon. It stained the clouds scattered in the sky a brilliant orange that faded in a few minutes. Afterward, all was gray, a gray that deepened into complete darkness. There was stars, but they didn't light objects more than a few feet away, and then dimly. If I avoided running right into one of the men hunting me, and if I avoided being skylighted on some ridge, I couldn't be seen by anyone.

I had the feeling it would be a good idea to avoid the Indians as well as the whites. The Indians certainly had reason to kill me now, and while some of them might not blame me, I couldn't count on all of them feeling that charitable.

I climbed out of the wash and headed straight away from the village. Then I realized that if I was going to survive out here all alone, I should have water and food. I hadn't had a drink for nearly twenty-four hours. Nor had I eaten in that length of time.

I turned and headed back toward the village, which still was smoldering. I should be able to find some kind of food that had not been burned. And I could drink my fill, which would give me another day or two to survive if I found no water during that time.

I walked as quietly as I could. The only sound was the rustling of the grass under my feet. I kept scanning the surrounding horizons, which was outlined against the sky, but I saw nothing that looked like a mounted man.

Once in a while I stopped to listen. I heard the yammering and barking of a pack of coyotes and I wondered if the sound was some kind of Indian signal. I'd always heard that Indians used the sounds of birds and animals as signals to each other.

I reached the edge of the village. The smoke was blowing straight into my face, and I began to choke and cough. Trying to stifle the cough, I headed around to the other side.

Over on that side there was, miraculously, one tepee that had not burned. It had started, and the lower part on one side was burned, but for some reason the fire had gone out. I stood there in front of it for several minutes, afraid to go in but knowing I had to if I was going to live.

Finally I got my courage up and stepped inside. It was as black as anything but I groped around, knowing from my short stay with the Indians where they kept their food. I found some bags made out of buffalo hides and felt in one of them to assure myself that it contained food. It was full of dried meat and I picked it up and carried it outside. Dried meat is hard to chew, but it's nourishing and what I had would last me a week or more.

I began to think that maybe I was going to get away. I had food, and as soon as I'd taken a good long drink at the stream, I'd head south toward Cheyenne. I knew one star, the north star, and if I headed away from it, eventually I ought to reach some kind of road leading into Cheyenne.

Maybe they'd be looking for me there, but it was a chance I had to take. I headed for the stream and walked out across its sandy bed to where the water ran. I put down the bag of dried meat and laid on my belly to drink. I drank until I felt bloated and then I got up.

A sound made me jump. It came from the direction of the village and it sounded like a horse stamping his feet. A chill ran along my spine. No horse could be in that burning village unless there was a man with him.

The first thing I thought was that maybe one had been tied in the village when it had been set ablaze. Instantly I remembered that there had been no horses in the village at the time of the attack.

My thoughts said, "Sligh," and I began to run. Sligh would have been clever enough to know that, if I was around, I'd return to the village for food.

He'd have no way of knowing, in the darkness, of course, that I wasn't just an Indian returning to recover what possessions remained unburned. But he'd check it out if he heard me or if he had seen me out on that white expanse of sand that formed the bed of the nearly dry stream.

I stopped running and crouched behind a clump of brush. I heard the horse's hoofbeats coming, at a steady walk as if his rider had all the time in the world.

They were approaching, so I knew Sligh had seen me. And then, shocking in the utter stillness, I heard his voice, "Better come out, kid. I know you're there. Sooner you come out the easier it's going to be for you."

I stopped breathing but I couldn't stop trembling. The brush behind which I crouched quivered and rustled faintly from my shaking but I doubted if Sligh could hear.

I could probably stay hidden as long as it was dark. But I couldn't cover any amount of ground. When daylight came, I'd be easy prey for him.

Instinctively I knew what was in store for me when

Sligh did catch up with me. A beating, the like of which I'd never got from Pa.

I thought of trying to fight. I thought of trying to get some kind of weapon. It would have to be a gun. Nothing else would even the odds between me and Sligh.

But there wasn't any guns. Not unless I could get Sligh off his horse and then circle around and get his rifle out of the saddle boot.

Deliberately I hit the brush with my hand. It made a noise loud enough to be heard. I froze then, and the horse stopped, not a dozen yards away from me.

Sligh's wheedling voice came, "Come on now, kid. I'll split the loot with you! We'll own that big damn' ranch together, just you an' me."

I heard the saddle creak as he swung from the horse's back. I heard his footsteps approaching.

I got up and ran. I ran as fast as I could for about a hundred yards. Then I stopped. I picked my way as carefully as I could at right angles to the direction I had been going. I crept along for another hundred yards and then turned back toward the place where Sligh had left his horse.

I was puzzled because I hadn't heard him running after me. He must be creeping along the way I had, I thought, listening for me and trying to make as little noise as possible.

I saw his horse looming up ahead, and I saw the stock of the rifle sticking up out of the saddle boot. Another fifteen yards, I thought, and then I'd have my hands on it.

CHAPTER 8

I was less than ten feet from the horse when I heard a sudden crashing of brush to my right and I knowed he'd outguessed me. Sligh was the right name for him. Damn him, he was as sly as a fox and he'd known I'd cither go for his horse or for his gun.

He hit me so hard he knocked me sprawling, but he kept his feet and the first thing I knew he was straddling me, holding me down, grappling for my hands to make sure I didn't have no weapons in them. Having made sure of that, he got to his feet, yanking me up along with him. He backhanded me alongside the face so hard it almost knocked me down again. I was mad, but I knew it wasn't going to do me no good to fight. Sligh was bigger, stronger, tougher and more experienced than I was. I wouldn't have minded fighting him if I'd had a chance, but I didn't. So I turned and ran. Maybe I could get away. Maybe I could hide like I had before. Maybe for once I could outthink him. It wasn't likely but it was the only chance I had.

I hadn't gone no more than a hundred yards before I heard his horse pounding toward me. I looked back as his loop sailed out. It settled over my head and I hit the end of the rope as his horse skidded to a halt. I hadn't figured that he could rope me in the dark, but there must of been enough light for it. I fell, and I heard him laugh. He said,

"Now, you little sonofabitch, let's see if we can't hammer some manners into you!"

But he didn't get off his horse. Instead he spurred the animal, jerking me behind at the end of the rope. I skidded along the ground, scratching my face and hands on brush clumps and rocks, tearing my clothes on the rocky ground. He spurred the horse into a gallop and the rope bit into my upper arms, which was pinned to my sides. I could hear him laughing and I hated him more bitterly and savagely than I had ever hated anything. But along with the hating was terror that the rope would slip up and close around my neck. If that happened, I'd be dead before Sligh could realize it, before he could stop dragging me.

I suppose my mad was the only thing that made me able to stand what was happening. Mad and hate. I wasn't thinking too good, but I knowed I would kill Sligh if it took me all the rest of my life. I would kill him, and I'd kill Donahue and maybe I'd kill the faithless bitch of a woman who had started all of this. I knowed that now he'd drag me until I was near dead and then he'd beat me with his fists. But none of that was going to change nothing. I'd kill him. Sooner or later. Only that promise to myself kept me hanging onto the rope, trying to protect myself as he dragged me in ever widening circles, laughing as if he enjoyed it all the time.

It went on and on, until my body was one great burning, bleeding mass, but it had to stop and finally it did. I laid there, choking on dust, not able to move or get up. It hurt to move and it hurt to lay still and I wondered if I was going to die. I didn't even hear Sligh's footsteps, but I felt him take the loop off me and then there was a short time while he coiled it and hung it on his saddle again. He came back, and yanked me to my feet, and hit me in the mouth with one of his fists.

Lips gave, and busted, and I tasted blood. I hoped he hadn't knocked out no teeth, but I was hurting too bad to worry much. I hit the ground on my back, damned if I was going to take any more without fighting back. I rolled and gathered knees and arms under me and I came up, running toward him with only some vague idea of trying to hurt him the way he was hurting me.

I drove my head into his belly and heard a big grunt of air drove from his lungs. He took a backward step, but like I said, he was strong and tough and experienced and he struck out instinctively, catching me on the side of the head with a glancing blow that almost tore loose an ear. I went down again, my head ringing. This time I felt a fist-sized rock with my hand and, grasping it, I came up again.

He was right over me. I swung the rock and heard it crack as it hit his head. He went to his knees and stayed there a moment, shaking his head. I rushed him again, swinging the rock, trying to finish him, but he ducked and the swing missed clean. He grabbed my arm and damn' near broke it twisting the rock out of my hand. Nearly out of his mind with fury, he held me with his left hand while he rained blows with his right into my face.

My nose busted, and my mouth was smashed again and again, and both of my eyes was hit so many times that they turned numb. I didn't want to quit, but I didn't have anything to say about it. Things began to whirl and bright lights flashed and I felt myself sinking into a pit of darkness and wondered if this was what dying was like.

I suppose if I'd stayed conscious, he might have beaten

me to death. The man was plumb out of his head. As it was he damn' near beat me to death and it was daylight and the sun was halfway up the sky before I came to. I couldn't see much when I did open my eyes, because both of them was swelled near shut. I could see a little light out of the slits, though, and the blurred figure of Sligh sitting on a rock and his horse beyond.

I struggled to sit up. Every movement caused so much pain that I caught my breath but I was damned if I was going to give him the satisfaction of hearing me groan or cry out with pain. This was worse than anything Pa had ever given me, but the idea was the same. Don't let them know they've hurt you and don't ever let them think they've broken you enough to make you beg.

He said, "Well. You've finally come out of it."

I didn't say nothing. I just looked at him and if he could have seen the hate in my eyes, he'd probably have beaten me again. He couldn't, though, because he couldn't see enough of them through the swelled and blackened flesh. I licked my smashed lips and winced with the pain it caused. I tried to speak, failed, and cleared my throat. I croaked, "What you goin' to do with me?"

He said, "Well, I'll kick the hell out of you again and again if that's what it takes. You'll do what I tell you to, or by God you'll end up dead. You got that straight?"

I said, "If I'm dead, you'll never get your hands on the Hunnicutt ranch."

I got to my feet, staggered and fell down again. I managed it up a second time, and this time I stayed up, swaying back and forth while the world reeled and tipped crazily. The sun was bright and the endless miles of Wyoming grassland stretched away to the horizons. I was thinking that it was a long ways to anyplace and that maybe my chance would come. If I could get Sligh's horse, it would leave him afoot and I'd be able to get away from him.

He had a fire going, and coffee on it in a blackened pot. He also had some canned beans that he'd heated. What was left of them had cooled, but I was hungry. He said, "Git yourself some coffee an' beans. Then we're goin' to go."

I stumbled to the fire. I drank coffee out of the pot, determined not to let the pain in my smashed mouth keep me from eating and drinking. I had to keep up my strength.

Chewing the cold beans hurt my mouth and I realized all my front teeth were loose. I'd had loose teeth before and they had always tightened up, so I didn't worry too much about them. My smashed mouth would heal, and the rest of me would heal, but if I had it out with Sligh again, I might not be alive when it was over with.

The thing for me to do was make him think he'd broken me. That might put him off his guard. I'd be meek and I'd do what he told me to, but I'd keep my eyes open and when my chance came I'd be ready for it. The way I felt right then, I could have killed him any way I could, by sticking a knife in his back while he slept, by leaving him alone and afoot out here, without food nor water, by beating him over the head with a rock until he was dead. He'd abused me so that where he was concerned, all the pity I might otherwise have felt was gone. He was a snake, poisonous and deadly, to be killed in any way possible.

He walked to his horse, after scrubbing out the fry pan with sand and dumping the coffee out. He tied them on, then beckoned me. "Come on."

I didn't hesitate. I walked to him and he mounted, then

put down his hand and pulled me up behind him. I almost cried out with the pain, but I gritted my teeth and didn't make a sound. I was behind him and the butt of his holstered revolver was staring me in the face. I thought of grabbing it and he must of known what was in my mind because he said, "Try it and you'll be on your ass on the ground before you can pull it clear."

He headed the horse south at a walk. From here we couldn't see the remains of the Indian village, but we could see a thin plume of smoke still raising from it far behind. Once, I saw a little group of Indians in a ravine around a tiny fire. They looked up, and watched us until we had gone past, but otherwise they didn't move.

I couldn't help thinking that a lot of innocent people was going to suffer for what Sligh and Donahue and the others had done to that little Cheyenne village. Indians, and whites too for that matter, go on the saying, "An eye for an eye and a tooth for a tooth." One way or another, them Cheyennes would have their revenge for what had been done to them. Trouble was, they wouldn't hit the ones who had killed their families. They'd hit isolated settlers, who hadn't done nothing to them at all.

The horse walked south. I was dizzy and weak, and I really didn't give a damn whether I lived or died. Except for the burning hunger for revenge. I'd live. And I'd kill Mr. Sligh. And when that was done I'd go back to Hunnicutt's and I'd kill Donahue and maybe Mrs. Hunnicutt.

We had gone several miles before I spoke. I said, "Where we going?"

"Denver."

"Why?"

"Well, takin' our time, it'll take maybe a week or so

gettin' there. It'll give you time to heal. I figger to git you some clothes. I figger to hire a lawyer and I figger on you inheritin' the Hunnicutt ranch. But not before you've signed over half of your interest in it to me. Or maybe a third to me and a third to the lawyer for gittin' it for us."

"What about the charge they got against me? Killin' Mr. Hunnicutt?"

He said, "First things first. Takes money to fight a thing like that. We git the right lawyer, an' he'll put up money to fight it out in court."

"Why Denver? Why not Cheyenne?"

"Well, I figger the folks in Cheyenne is likely partial to Wyoming cattlemen. Might be a chore to git a lawyer that'd do what we want him to."

I tried to relax, only bracing myself against the back of the saddle enough to keep from getting hurt too badly when the horse went down into a gully or climbed out of it.

We didn't stop at noon and I didn't care because it hurt so much to eat I wasn't anxious to try doing it again so soon. All afternoon we plodded south while the heat increased. Heat made my hurts even worse. All I wanted to do was lie down and close my eyes and die. But I hung on, clinging to the cantle of the saddle and wishing to God the time would pass quickly so we could stop. Maybe with a good night's sleep, I'd be stronger and able to go on.

Sligh found a little grove of cottonwoods on the bank of a stream near sundown and stopped. I slid off without being told and promptly fell. I got up and leaned against one of the trees while Sligh unsaddled and watered and picketed his horse. Turning, he saw me leaning against the tree and snarled, "Git some wood, you lazy little sonofabitch! You think I'm goin' to wait on you?"

I lowered my glance so he wouldn't see my eyes. Oh God, I thought, it's going to be sweet killin' you! I staggered away and began picking up sticks of wood. Bending and stooping hurt so bad it was all I could do to keep from crying out. But I never made a sound, and after a while I went back to where Sligh was, a big load of firewood in my arms.

He snarled, "Build a fire!"

I said, "Yes, sir," and knelt down and began to break off some of the smaller twigs. I built a little tepee with them, and added larger sticks and he threw me a match and I lighted it. He said, "Water. Git water in the coffeepot an' fill my canteen."

He was sitting on the ground comfortably with his back to a cottonwood. I took the coffeepot and canteen from his saddle and carried them to the stream.

I'd never known it before, but I was discovering that hate can be pleasurable. You can hate so hard and strong that you begin to enjoy your hate.

That was the way it was with me. I looked back at him as if my eyes could burn a hole in him.

CHAPTER 9

I supposed the posse under Donahue had gone back, probably having decided I had been either killed by the Indians or killed in the attack on their village. But we still had to pass near Cheyenne on our way to Denver and I was pretty sure the sheriff there, and maybe a U.S. marshal too, would be on the lookout for anyone that looked like me. Mr. Hunnicutt had been an important man. They wouldn't give up easy in their search for the one supposed to have murdered him.

Sligh, maybe thinking the same thing, made a wide circle around Cheyenne. But it wasn't wide enough. One morning we waked up to find a dozen men standing over us, holding guns. One, a big raw-boned man with long hair and a wide straw-colored mustache wore a U.S. marshal's badge. His voice was as big as the rest of him and he said, "All right, boys, roll out. Stand up an' let's see who you are."

I stumbled to my feet, wincing with the pain. I wondered what kind of story Sligh was going to tell, but I knew from the still way his face was that he was scared. He stretched and stirred the dead fire with his toe and said, "Mornin', boys. What brings you out here this time of mornin'?"

The marshal said, "I'm Sam Gurd. We're lookin' for a killer."

Sligh grinned at him in that sly way of his and said, "Well now, do we look like killers to you?"

Gurd didn't answer him. He was studying me pretty close and at last he asked, "What happened to you, boy? You look like you tangled with a mountain lion."

Sligh didn't give me time to answer. He broke in: "He was catched by some Cheyenne Indians. Me an' some others come to rescue him an' we had a tussle with the redskins gettin' him away. I reckon they figgered we was after the boy an' so they beat him up pretty bad afore we got to him."

Gurd looked skeptical. "Don't sound like Cheyennes, beatin' a boy like that."

Sligh said, "You don't think I'd beat him, do you?"

Gurd walked over to him. Sligh didn't have his gun. It was laying on the ground beside his bed. Gurd said, "Let's see your hands."

Sligh held them out, palms up. Gurd said, "No. Turn 'em over."

Sligh did. Gurd didn't have to examine them closely to see how skinned the knuckles were. He looked Sligh square in the eye and said, "You're a liar, mister. You beat that boy."

Sligh tried to meet his glance and failed. He looked at the ground and scuffed his toe and finally he said defensively, "Well, by God, I got a right. He's my boy an' he's a runaway. Man's got a right to catch an' bring back his own flesh an' blood."

Gurd said, "Ain't got no right to beat him half to death. Ain't got no right to drag him, neither."

Sligh said, "Horse gave me a time. Couldn't hold him for a spell after I roped the boy."

Gurd turned to me. "What's your story, boy?"

Well, I knew if I told the truth, the marshal would take me and throw me in his jail. There wasn't a chance I could prove I didn't kill Hunnicutt, not with his widow and his foreman claiming they was eyewitnesses. So it was a choice between going to jail for a long time and maybe hanging for murder or putting up with Sligh's meanness. It wasn't much of a choice. I said, "It's true. I run away an' he caught up with me."

Gurd plainly didn't believe neither me or Sligh. He scowled for a long time. Finally he asked, "Where you bound?"

"Denver. That's where we live. Boy run away from there. Cheyennes caught him south of here an' I followed their trail to where they was camped."

"Who was the others that helped you out?"

"Freighters. Had a train of wagons headin' for Laramie."

Gurd nodded. He said, "All right. But I'm followin' your trail north a ways, an' if I find out you been lyin' to me, I'm comin' after you."

Sligh looked mighty relieved. He said, "Fair enough, Marshal. Fair enough."

The marshal mounted up, gave Sligh a parting scowl and rode away, heading north. The others followed him.

Sligh stood there watching until the bunch rode out of sight over a knoll. Then he moved and fast. He said, "Come on. Pick up the stuff while I saddle up my horse."

He hurried out to where the horse was picketed. I rolled up the blankets and picked up the coffeepot and fry pan and put them in their greasy gunnysack. I was stiff, and I still hurt, but I felt better than I had yesterday.

He tied the stuff on, mounted, then put down a hand and helped me up behind. He took out, with the horse at a steady, mile-eating trot, a gait that might be easy on the horse but that was hell on me. I bounced up and down on the horse's rump and every time I came down I felt like crying out. I gritted my teeth and stayed still, though, because I'd made up my mind I was going to bide my time. I didn't want to make Sligh mad at me no more because if he beat me now on top of the old hurts it would be unbearable. I'd do just what he said and I wouldn't look at him because if I did he'd see what was in my eyes.

Gurd was eventually going to find out that Sligh had lied. He'd find no trail of freighters' wagons heading for Laramie. Instead he'd find the trail of Donahue and the posse from Hunnicutt's and he'd find the dead Indians and the burned village, in itself a crime in the eyes of the government in Washington. He'd put two and two together and come to the conclusion that I was the one being hunted for killing Mr. Hunnicutt. Once he figured that far, he'd come after us as damn' fast as he could ride.

Sligh didn't even try to hide his trail. He just lit out straight for Denver, and late that afternoon we hit the Platte and got into the road, and after that there wasn't much chance of anybody picking up our trail. There were stagecoaches and wagons and horsemen on the road and in a matter of an hour or so every one of our horse's tracks would be blotted out.

Sligh pulled off the road where the grass was high about dark that night, and we laid down and slept for four or five hours. Then we rode again, and at noon the next day we rode into Denver.

It was the biggest town I ever saw. And the busiest. Wagons rolling down the streets raised big clouds of dust that hung in between the buildings so thick you sometimes couldn't see a block. I guessed it was the first time Sligh had been here too because he gawked at the tall buildings just the way I did. He kept saying over and over, "Well, by God, I wouldn't a believed it if I hadn't seen it with my own two eyes."

They had horse-drawn streetcars to carry people back and forth and besides them and the wagons there was lots of fancy buggies and surreys shining black with bright yellow wheels whirling along behind high-stepping slick-looking horses.

There was people dressed a way I'd never seen before. Women in fancy long dresses carryin' parasols to keep the sun off their faces and men in handsome gray and black broadcloth suits with top hats or round-topped hats they called derbies.

But there was plenty of people like us too, kids runnin' around ragged and barefoot and women in dark, worn clothes with shawls over their heads carryin' market baskets from the stores. There was lots of workingmen, in work clothes and they all went about their business without so much as lookin' at each other.

Sligh rode aimlessly up and down the streets, looking at everything. I was hungry and tired, and I hurt all over but I didn't say nothing because I knowed it wouldn't do no good. But I did get the idea that maybe in a place like this I could get away from Sligh. Come dark, I'd try, unless he tied my hands or locked me in a room to keep me from trying to get away.

Pretty soon we came to a little shack stuck between two big new brick buildings. There was a sign in the window of the place that said, A. ROUSCH, ATTY. AT LAW. I didn't know what the "Atty." meant, but I understood the word "law." Sligh turned his horse in to the tie rail and told me to get down. I did, debating in my mind whether to run or not. I decided against it. People here was probably against runaways just like they was every place else, and I was too stiff and sore to run very fast. When I did make my try at getting away, I wanted as good a chance as it was possible for me to get.

Sligh said, "Come on," and we went through a sagging picket gate and up a dirt walk to the door of the place. Sligh knocked and a voice inside said, "Come on in," and we went inside.

It was dark and musty-smelling and there was more books around the place than I'd ever seen before. There was a man sitting behind a tall roll-top desk, and he peered around the side of it with spectacles pinched to his long hooked nose and said, "Well, what is it? What do you want?"

Sligh said, "Name's Hank Sligh. This here is Jason Ord."

"All right. What do you want?"

"You're a lawyer, ain't you?"

"Says so on the sign, don't it?"

"Yes, sir." Sligh dug in his pocket and pulled out the paper Mr. Hunnicutt had signed, giving his ranch to me in case he died. He unfolded it and spread it out so's the lawyer could see, but he didn't let go of it. Rousch reached for it but Sligh yanked it back. Rousch said, "What is it?

If you don't want me to see it, then get out of here, both of you."

Sligh said, "We may look raggedy, Mr. Lawyer, but this here's a will givin' this boy one of the biggest damn' ranches in Wyoming Territory. If you don't want to talk about it, then by God we can find some other lawyer who sure as hell will."

The lawyer got up from behind his desk. His irritable manner was gone suddenly and he came around to Sligh and said in a voice that had turned polite, "I'm sorry, Mr. Sligh. Of course I'm interested in helping you. Won't you both sit down?" He dragged a couple of chairs from the corner of the room and Sligh and me sat down.

Rousch kept his eyes on the paper in Sligh's hand. He said, "You said something about a will. May I see it please?"

Sligh hesitated, but finally he handed Rousch the will. The lawyer read it quickly. He looked up. "There are no witnesses."

Sligh said sourly, "Course not. There ain't usually a batch of witnesses out in the middle of the Wyoming cattle range. That's where it was wrote."

The lawyer said doubtfully, "Well, I don't know. A will without witnesses . . ."

Sligh reached over and snatched the paper away from him. He got up. "All right. If you don't think . . ."

Rousch didn't let him finish. He said quickly, "I didn't say I didn't think it was legitimate. Just tell me what the problem is. Is somebody contesting this boy's right to inherit the ranch?"

Sligh said, "Just about everybody, that's all. You don't

think I'd be talkin' to you if all he had to do was walk in and take over the place, do you?"

"What *is* the problem, Mr. Sligh?"

"He's wanted for murder, that's what. He's accused of killin' Mr. Hunnicutt so's he could inherit Mr. Hunnicutt's ranch."

Rousch took a long look at me, shaking his head. "So young," he clucked. "Did you do it, boy?"

"Course not," I said. "Why would I want to kill Mr. Hunnicutt? He saved my life an' he give me a job."

"Know who did kill him?"

I said, "The foreman, Mr. Donahue. Mr. Hunnicutt caught him with Mrs. Hunnicutt an' Mr. Donahue shot him dead."

Rousch said, "Ah, that. And now Donahue and Mrs. Hunnicutt are hunting you and Donahue probably will arrange it so that you're killed before you're brought to trial?"

Sligh said, "That's it."

Rousch shook his head doubtfully. "I don't know," he said. "A will without witnesses. And a boy accused of killing his benefactor."

Sligh got up. He said, "Come on, Jason."

Rousch said, "Wait a minute, Mr. Sligh. Is Jason your son?"

Sligh shook his head. He said, "I he'ped him. When they was chasin' him, I he'ped him get away."

I didn't argue, because there wasn't any use wasting my breath. Rousch said in a voice that was as slick as windmill grease, "Then you're also his benefactor, aren't you, Mr. Sligh? You're only interested in what is good for this boy."

Sligh looked puzzled. "You might say that."

"What happened to him? He looks like he'd tangled with . . ."

Sligh said, "Indians. They captured him. I he'ped get him away."

Rousch nodded, but he knew what had happened to me. He said, "All right, Mr. Sligh. I'll take your case. For a third of the Hunnicutt ranch when we get our hands on it. Come back in an hour, and I'll have the papers for you to sign."

Sligh nodded doubtfully and pushed me toward the door. We went out. It was like being in partnership with a pair of wolves, I thought. In the end, one of the three of us would own Hunnicutt's ranch and it wasn't going to be me. I'd be dead and so would either Rousch or Sligh.

CHAPTER 10

We walked from the lawyer's office to the nearest hotel, with Sligh leading his horse. I gave the town a good looking over without letting Sligh catch me at it. If I was going to get away from him, this was the placc for it. There was a thousand places to hide in a city as big as this and he couldn't trail me here, that was surc.

But I didn't bolt. Not yet. As stiff and sore as I was, I knew I couldn't outrun him. He couldn't watch me twenty-four hours a day, though, and eventually a chance would come. When it did, I'd be ready for it.

We got a room at an old, frame hotel that sagged and lookcd as if it would fall down first time a good wind hit it. We climbed the rickety stairs, carrying saddle and saddlebags and blanket roll and the gunnysack holding the blackened pans and what little food was left.

Sligh locked the door as we went out again, and I followed him down the stairs. We walked around aimlessly until the hour had passed. Then we went back to Rousch's office. He had the papers all ready for us to sign.

I had to sign a last will and testament giving everything I owned to Sligh and Rousch in equal shares. After that, I had to sign another paper giving Rousch a third interest in the ranch, and I had to sign one giving Sligh a third. After that, he had to sign a will leaving everything he owned to Rousch. Rousch signed a similar will leaving his share in the Hunnicutt ranch to Sligh.

It was a devilish bargain struck between two thieves. They would clear me of the murder charge because they had to in order for me to inherit the Hunnicutt ranch. But I wouldn't live much more than a day or two afterward. I'd meet with some kind of accident, and that would leave Rousch and Sligh in sole possession of the big Hunnicutt ranch.

Even as sore as I was, I could still smile thinking of what would happen afterward. Each would be trying to kill the other in such a way that the finger of guilt wouldn't point him out. In the end, maybe both would die.

As soon as all the papers was signed, Sligh tucked his copies into his pocket and we headed back to the hotel. I went into the room and Sligh closed the door behind me, locking it.

I heard his footsteps going down the stairs. As soon as I couldn't hear them no more, I went to the window and looked out. I was on the third floor and it was at least twenty-five, maybe thirty feet to the ground. If I tried to jump, I'd break a leg, even if the fall didn't kill me. Jumping from the window was out of the question.

I went to the door and tried it, but it was locked. I hunted around for something to use as a key, but I couldn't find nothing.

The window faced the street. I went back to it and saw Sligh walking along leading his horse. He disappeared into the open doorway of a livery stable and showed up a few minutes later without the horse.

Rousch met him there in front of the livery stable. They both turned and looked up at the window where I was, and Sligh pointed. I ducked back even though I was sure that neither of them could see me there. The window was dirty and the sun was shining on it and it would be impossible to see anything through it from the street.

They turned and walked away, finally turning in the door of a small, one-room building. There was a high pole behind the building, and telegraph wires leading away from it. Rousch wasn't losing no time, I thought. He must be telegraphing the sheriff in Cheyenne. I had no way of knowing what he'd be saying in the telegram, but he was probably telling the sheriff that he had information in the death of Mr. Hunnicutt and would the sheriff get in touch with him.

He was playing a pretty dangerous game because the sheriff in Cheyenne was hand in glove with the big cattle interests. The first thing *he'd* do would be to send someone out to the Hunnicutt ranch to tell Donahue about the telegram. Maybe he'd come to Denver, afterward, to talk to Rousch. But Donahue would come too, bringing those of his crew he could count on to do exactly what he told them to. They'd turn Denver upside down, looking for me, and they sure wasn't going to take me alive. Only if I was dead could Donahue be sure him and Mrs. Hunnicutt wasn't going to be charged with the murder of Mr. Hunnicutt. Only my death could close the case. I didn't know whether Donahue knew about the will Mr. Hunnicutt had left or not. He probably did not, unless Sligh had let it slip. But if he did, he'd have even more reason to want me dead.

In the risky game Sligh and Rousch were playing it was my life that was at stake. I just had to get away.

For a little while I walked nervously back and forth.

Finally I decided I was tiring myself and getting more upset and nervous all the time. I hadn't done much sleeping the last few days and I was plumb worn out. If I was going to get away from Sligh and keep Donahue from finding me, I'd better get rested so I could keep going when there was need for it.

I laid down on the bed and closed my eyes. I went to sleep right away and did not awake until Sligh came in the door. He had some bread with him, and cheese, and a pitcher of water he'd brought up from downstairs. He put the things down and said, "There. Go ahead and eat."

My first impulse was to tell him to go to hell, but that wouldn't help me and it sure wouldn't hurt him. I got off the bed and helped myself to the bread and cheese, washing it down with water. He said, "You need to go to the outhouse?"

I nodded, and when I had finished eating, he unlocked the door and followed me down the stairs. I wanted to find out where the back door of the hotel was and I wanted to see the lay of the land behind the hotel. There was two outhouses, one for men and the other for women. Beyond was a shed, where firewood was stored, and beyond that an alley. Shacks were scattered along the alley, some in use as stables, some as storage sheds. There was several board fences along the alley, most of them sagging and ready to fall down, and there was a lot of empty tin cans and trash lying around.

I went to the outhouse and then Sligh herded me back into the hotel and up the stairs to the room. He locked me in again, and again I laid down on the bed. Sleep came just as easy as it had the last time and I did not wake up until the room was dark.

I went to the window and looked out. There was lights along the street, some in windows, some on buggies moving back and forth along the street. I tried the door, hoping Sligh had forgotten to lock it, but he had not.

I wondered how long it would take the sheriff in Cheyenne and Donahue to get to Denver. I guessed the distance was around a hundred miles. If they was in enough of a hurry, they could make it overnight. I'd heard of men on horseback covering more than a hundred and fifty miles in a day and night.

So they could get here any time after daylight tomorrow, and I had better be gone when they did get here if I wanted to go on living for a while.

Sligh figured he was so damned sly, I thought, and Rousch thought he had stumbled onto a fortune, but neither of them was a match for Donahue. He had his back to the wall and was facing only two choices. If he got rid of me, and Sligh, Mrs. Hunnicutt would inherit the Hunnicutt ranch and he could marry her, this way getting it for himself. But if Sligh and Rousch made my claim to the ranch hold up, Donahue would lose not only Mrs. Hunnicutt and the ranch but he'd probably hang for killing Mr. Hunnicutt to boot.

With this kind of choice facing him, I didn't figure he'd fool around. Sligh should have known it too. He lived up there in Wyoming Territory on the boundary of the Hunnicutt ranch. He knew the way the big ranchers treated anybody that stood up to them.

Still, lying here worrying wasn't going to change nothing. What I'd better do was get as much sleep as I could. Time and rest would heal my hurts. When the time came for traveling, for running and hiding, I ought to be as ready for it as possible.

Sligh came in about midnight. I knowed he had been drinking because I could smell it on him and because he staggered and almost fell down between the door and the bed. I was sleeping in my clothes so I'd be ready to run if I got a chance. He had locked the door, and, I guess, had put the key in his pocket. He collapsed on the bed, and was snoring almost right away.

I waited a little while to be sure he was sound asleep. He was lying on his stomach, so I felt in his back pockets first. The key wasn't in either one of them. He stirred as I felt in the second back pocket and turned, taking a swipe at me with one of his hands. It missed.

I waited a long time afterward. I didn't want to wake him because being drunk, no telling what he'd do to me. But neither did I want to give up and just wait for tomorrow when Donahue and the Cheyenne sheriff would arrive.

I felt carefully for his right-hand front pocket, but he was lying on it and I couldn't get my hand in it. He stirred, grumbled a curse, and took another swipe at me.

I'd have to wait, I realized, until maybe he turned over on his back. Then maybe I would have a chance of going through his pockets without waking him.

I laid awake all the rest of the night, waiting for him to turn, but he never did. He laid there like a log on his stomach, snoring off and on, stinking of the whisky that he'd drunk.

Dawn came gray and cold-looking and finally the sun came up. I'd been lying there for a good many hours, so I got up and walked back and forth across the room, loosening up my muscles. I felt a lot better than I had the day before. I felt, for the first time since the beating he'd given me, that I could run, that maybe I could get away. But first I had to get out of this room.

I was hungry, but it was going to be a while before I got anything to eat. I stood at the window staring down for a long, long time.

I didn't see nobody come into the hotel but I heard somebody climbing the stairs and a little while afterward someone knocked on the door. I supposed that it was Rousch.

Sligh didn't stir. Rousch knocked louder and louder until finally he was banging on the door with his fist.

Sligh groaned, and cursed, and rolled over. He finally got to a sitting position and growled, "What the hell's going on?"

I said, "Mr. Rousch is at the door."

"Then let him in, you little sonofabitch."

"I can't. I ain't got the key."

He fumbled in his pocket for the key. He threw it to me and I crossed the room and stuck it into the lock.

I knowed this was my chance to get away. Sligh was half asleep and Rousch would be too surprised to do anything for a minute or two.

I turned the key and opened the door. But it wasn't Rousch who stood in the doorway looking at me. It was Donahue and behind him was another man wearing a silver star on his vest.

I didn't take time to wonder how they'd known which hotel we was in. Maybe Sligh had mentioned its name in his telegram. Panic hit me and I drove out the door, knocking Donahue aside and ducking past the sheriff. I was clear, and I ran like a rabbit for the stairs.

Behind me, Donahue yelled, "Hey, you little bastard!" and fired a shot that sounded like the end of the world in the narrow hallway. The sheriff yelled after me too, but I was halfway down the stairs.

The trip yesterday to the outhouse sure helped me now. I ducked down the hallway leading to the back door of the hotel and busted through it before Donahue and the sheriff reached the foot of the stairs. There hadn't been a clerk at the desk and this early in the morning no one had been sitting in the lobby. There'd be no one to tell them which way I'd gone and they'd likely suppose I had gone out the front.

I sprinted across the yard behind the hotel. The door of the men's outhouse was open and I could see a man sitting there. He looked startled and closed the door. I reached the alley, stumbled on a pile of tin cans and fell, skinning knees and elbows, but I was up again before the racket of the tin cans had quit, and was heading down the alley as fast as I could run.

My stiff, sore muscles seemed to loosen up as I ran. I couldn't hear nothing behind me but I thought I heard shouting, probably in front of the hotel.

I thought, You've made it, and there was some excitement in knowing that I had but I wasn't out of the woods yet, not by a long shot. I still had to find a place to hide and it was daylight so almost anyplace I went someone would see me go there and be around to say so later when Donahue and Sligh and the sheriff started prowling through the town.

Early as it was, there was a good many people on the street. They turned to stare at me as I ran past.

The first thing to do, I thought, would be to get off the street. Get into the alleys, where there wasn't no people.

I ducked down the first one I reached. Denver had seemed big to me yesterday. Today it seemed too small, as I looked frantically for a safe place to hide.

CHAPTER 11

Down at the other end of the alley, a bunch of men crossed, talking among themselves. I hid myself in a doorway, hoping I had not been seen. Those men wasn't looking for me but if they saw me they'd remember it later if they was asked by someone who was.

With people around it was too late to run through the streets. I had to hide, here, now, in this alley before somebody saw me who could later give me away.

There was a loading dock about halfway between me and the alley's end. It wasn't perfect, but it was a place to hide. I ran to it and ducked underneath.

The dock was built of planks and was supported by stout log sections set firmly in the ground. It had turned into a kind of collection place for trash. Everything lying in the alley and in the way had been tossed under it.

That trash offered me a chance. I burrowed into it, and rats scurried away as I moved in on them. I hated rats and was half afraid of them, but I poked one that showed fight with a stick and he ran too.

Now I began fixing the loose boards in front of me, trying to make the pile look natural while making myself a good hiding place behind it. It was dusty and hot and the place was loaded with cobwebs. Finally I felt as if I was safe, at least unless someone stooped and peered underneath the dock. Which wasn't likely.

I didn't get finished none too soon. A wagon drawn by two big bays came rattling into the alley. It stopped in front of the dock. The teamster got down and pounded on the back door and pretty soon someone opened it. The teamster unloaded several boxes on the dock, spoke to his team and drove away.

Dirt sifted down on me as the man above carried the boxes, one by one, into the store. The door slammed, was bolted, and all was quiet again.

It was going to take Donahue a while to get organized, I supposed, but he had plenty of money. He could hire a hundred men if he wanted to. Both his life and that of Mrs. Hunnicutt was at stake. She wouldn't hesitate to spend a few thousand dollars finding me if it saved her neck.

I dozed, waking up when a second wagon came down the alley, this one drawn by two teams of blacks. It was loaded high with beer kegs and it stopped behind a saloon farther down the alley. The driver unloaded half a dozen kegs, received his pay and drove on again.

A couple of men came sidling down the alley, their eyes shifting back and forth, talking in whispers between themselves. One looked at the dock where I was hiding for what seemed to me to be a long, long time. A pair of thieves, I thought, looking for something that wasn't nailed down. They went on, looking at each door to see if it was open.

They passed my hiding place. The one who had studied the dock so long looked back at it. I froze, hardly daring to breathe. I wondered if he'd seen me and decided he had not. If he had, he'd have investigated because if I'd been dead or drunk there would have been a possibility of robbing me.

The two disappeared and it was half an hour before anybody else came into the alley. When they did, I knew I was in trouble. I didn't know either one of them and I didn't think they were Hunnicutt hands, but they was looking for somebody and I figured it was me. They checked every door. They looked into passageways between buildings, and from one they dragged a pile of trash to see if anybody was under it.

My hiding place was no good no more. I knew that right away. They'd drag out the boards and trash I was hiding behind and they'd have me. I wouldn't have a chance of getting away from two of them once they'd gotten their hands on me.

I just didn't have no choice. I dug out of the trash pile beneath the dock on the side away from the men. They must of seen something move, because they came running toward the dock.

I jumped out and sprinted for the alley mouth. Behind me, one of the men yelled, "Hey you! Stop!"

I only ran faster. The other man yelled, "I'll shoot!"

I thought, Oh Lord, and began dodging back and forth from one side of the alley to the other as I ran. A gun racketed behind me and a bullet kicked up a spurt of dust thirty or forty feet ahead of me.

Damn it, that suddenly made me mad. Sligh had dragged me and beat me and I'd been hounded just about long enough. It was time I started fighting back, for all I was only sixteen years old and not too stout. There was ways a body could fight back when somebody was doin' dirt to him.

There was likely a U.S. marshal in a town this big. And a U.S. marshal is supposed to be honest and working on the side of the law. Sheriffs and town marshals could be crooked but U.S. marshals was supposed to be different.

Running wasn't no good. I'd been running long enough to know that by now. Standing and fighting would only get me killed. I needed somebody on my side.

I ran out into the street, with the two yelling after me. I crossed the street, crowded with wagons, buggies, horsemen and people walking, dodging this way and that to avoid bumping into them. One man reached out and tried to grab me but I pulled away.

I ducked into a passageway between two buildings. It was scattered with tin cans and trash, but I cat-footed it over them and when I reached the end of the alley I saw some stairs leading up to the second floor of the building on my right.

I ran up the stairs, reaching the top as I heard the men kicking the tin cans in the passageway. I tried the door at the head of the stairs. It was unlocked so I went in.

The room I went into was empty. It was full of dust and there was cobwebs at the window. I raised the window. There was an awning right below. I squeezed out of the window and lowered myself until my feet touched the awning. I let go then and slid down the awning and dropped to the boardwalk underneath.

I was up and running before the surprised people who had seen me drop could open their mouths. Crossing the street I went into another passage between buildings, ran along an alley and came out onto another street.

People turned to stare at me. It was because of the Indian clothes, I guessed. They was ragged and dirty on top of that, and I hadn't washed for days. Besides that, I'd been burrowing under that dusty dock all morning and the dirt from that was all over me.

This was a big town and I might look for the marshal's office a long time before I found it. I figured I'd better ask somebody. I stopped running, but I kept a sharp lookout for anybody that might be taking an interest in me.

Out in the middle of one of the streets there was a stone fountain, with troughs for horses to drink out of. I went out there and washed up good in one of the horse troughs. I brushed as much of the dirt off my clothes as I could. I went on afterward and as soon as I was dry, I stopped a man and said, "Scuse me, mister, but I'm lookin' for the U.S. marshal's office. You know where it is?"

He looked at me. He said, "You a runaway, kid?"

I said, "No, sir. My folks is dead. Killed by the Injuns gettin' here."

"What you want the marshal for?"

I did some fast thinking and said, "They won't give me the horses an' wagon that belonged to my folks. I figure the marshal could get 'em for me."

The answer seemed to satisfy him. He pointed. "You go up that way four blocks an' turn right. It's about half-way down the block on your right."

I said, "Thanks, mister," and hurried away.

I didn't run, but I walked as fast as I could. I tried not to look like somebody was chasing me, but I sure studied everybody I saw comin' toward me. I finally reached the right corner and turned and ahead I saw a little square stone building with bars at the windows. There was a sign out front that said, U. S. MARSHAL.

I was scared, but I tried the door. It was locked. I looked

around. There was people on the street here too and I knew that if Donahue had hired a lot of men, sooner or later some of them would come by here. I'd have to get out of sight, at least. I looked around, trying to find a place I could hide and see the marshal's office too.

There was a building across the street. Someone must have been working on the roof because there was a ladder leaning against the building. I crossed the street, trying to look businesslike and as if I knew what I was doing. I climbed the ladder to the roof.

The building was only one story but it had a high false front to make it look bigger than it really was. I was able to get up behind that false front and sit down. I could look around one end of it and see the marshal's office and there wasn't much chance that anybody would see me.

It was like maybe the Lord had felt sorry for me and was finally beginning to help me out. I hoped he stayed with me, because by now I knew I needed all the help that I could get.

I sat down, thinking about Mr. Hunnicutt. He'd been the first man I'd ever met who had helped me without figuring on getting anything out of it himself. Just because he was a real good man. Just because he liked me and wanted to help me out.

I'd seen him killed. And I owed it to him to see that the two who had killed him paid for what they'd done and didn't profit by getting the big ranch he'd spent his life building up.

I wasn't greedy and I'd never had enough to know what it was like to own something, but what I did know was that Mr. Hunnicutt had scrawled a will leaving the ranch he'd built to me because he didn't want to leave it to his faithless wife.

The sun climbed up the sky. Being summer, it got pretty hot, especially on this roof where the sun hit it and bounced back up against me so that I got it from both up and down. I waited for a long, long time. Finally I saw Donahue and another man with a shiny silver star on his vest coming down the street. They stopped at the marshal's office, tried the door, then stood there talking for a while before they went on again.

I relaxed when they disappeared around the corner. It wasn't very long before Sligh and Rousch came down the street. They stopped at the marshal's office too and tried the door. Afterward they too went on down the street and disappeared.

A long time went by. Finally I saw a man stop at the door of the marshal's office. He had a key, and he unlocked the door.

He was a stocky man, but close to six feet tall, and because of the way he was built, he must have weighed well over two hundred pounds. He had a wide mustache that swept down away from his mouth, curling up at the ends. It was the color of fresh-thrashed straw, just like his hair was underneath his hat. He wore a pistol in a leather holster at his side, and the belt that held it was full of cartridges in loops made to hold them.

He wore high-heeled Texas boots and a vest above his pants, where his badge was pinned. It wasn't shiny like the Cheyenne sheriff's badge. It was tarnished and dull and to see it you had to look real close.

He unlocked the door and went inside. I was so scared I could hardly swallow and my knees was shaking so bad

I could hardly get down the ladder to the street. I told myself I was a damn' fool for going to the law because so far all the law had given me was trouble and there wasn't no reason to think it was going to change.

Still, I knew getting help was the only chance I had. Donahue's men would kill me on sight, and Sligh and Rousch had the same fate in mind for me, only later when I'd inherited the Hunnicutt ranch and had taken it over.

I crossed the street. I looked up and down it for Donahue and the sheriff and for Sligh and Rousch, but I didn't see any of them. I opened the door and went inside.

The marshal looked up from behind a big roll-top desk. Suddenly I was even more scared than I had been before. The marshal stood up, towering over me. He was so big and overpowering that I felt like running away. He seemed to know how I felt, though, and said in a deep, easy voice, "Hello, boy. What can I do for you?"

I groped around for the right thing to say. Finally I said, "I'm Jason Ord."

The marshal came across the room and stuck out his hand. I took it and it was so big it wrapped around mine like a blanket. He said, "I'm Frank Rittenhouse, U.S. marshal for this territory."

I said, "You ain't going to believe what I tell you, but it's the truth."

He said, "How you know I ain't going to believe? You try me, Jason. If you're tellin' the truth, why I'll believe."

I didn't know whether he would or not. The story I had to tell him was so wild that I didn't see how anybody could believe. The side Donahue and the Cheyenne sheriff would tell was a whole lot more believable.

But I'd come this far and there wasn't nothing to do now but go on with it. Besides that, if I tried to get away, he'd catch me. Up against a man like this here U.S. marshal, I wouldn't have a chance.

CHAPTER 12

For a couple of minutes I stood there, trying to figure out the best way to begin. I had to make this marshal believe me. My life depended on it. He waited, but finally he said, "Just start at the beginning, son. And tell the truth."

Well, it wasn't no time to tell part of the truth, so I said, "I run away from home. My pa was always beatin' me, an' I got tired of it. I takened an old horse he had an' food to last me a couple of days an' I lit out."

He didn't say anything. I said, "I traveled by night an' I stole to eat. Eggs out of henhouses and bread that had been set out to cool. I never got seen and I got to Wyoming Territory before my horse finally laid down and died. After that I walked. I didn't have no food and I began to get weak. Finally I figured I'd come to the end of the line. I laid down to sleep knowin' I was going to die."

I thought maybe he'd say something, or ask me where I'd run away from, but he didn't. I said, "When I woke up, there was Mr. Hunnicutt looking down at me. He give me somethin' to eat, and some water, and he talked to me. He said he'd been a runaway hisself and he wasn't going to turn me in. He said I could come with him and be the chore boy on his ranch. If I worked out, he reckoned later I could be a cowboy if I wanted to.

"There wasn't nothing else for me to do but go with him.

He helped me up on his horse and we rode to his ranch. A man named Donahue, that was his foreman, put me in the bunkhouse an' told me where to get something to eat. And I went to work."

The marshal nodded. "All right so far. Don't worry about the runaway thing, son. I ain't going to send you back."

I said, "I'm into somethin' a lot worse than running away."

"All right. Go on."

"Well, Mr. Donahue was in the house a lot with Mrs. Hunnicutt when Mr. Hunnicutt was gone. One night I got up to go to the outhouse. I seen Mr. Hunnicutt ride in like there was some hell of a hurry. He jumped off his horse and went into the house. I heard some yelling and then some shots and I went and looked into the kitchen window. Mr. Hunnicutt was on the floor with blood all over him and Mr. Donahue was standing there with a gun smoking in his hand. I backed off, but I stumbled over a bucket and fell down, making a lot of racket when I did. They come out after me and I knowed they'd kill me sure to shut me up about what I'd seen. There wasn't nothing to do but run, so I jumped on Mr. Hunnicutt's horse and lit out, with them raising hell back in the yard about how I'd killed Mr. Hunnicutt."

The marshal said, "That was a fix, son, an' you with nothing but your underwear. What'd you do?"

"Well, I found me a shack, and rode up to it, figuring I might get me something to put on and some food. A rifle poked out of the window and I was scared to run. A man came out and made me get down. He had some Hunnicutt cattle in his corral and he drove 'em out and hid my trail coming to his place. He turned Mr. Hunnicutt's horse loose and took me back to his place on his horse with him."

"Who was this man?"

"His name is Mr. Sligh. He went through Mr. Hunnicutt's saddlebags before he turned the horse loose and he found a piece of paper writ by Mr. Hunnicutt leaving his ranch to me."

I was watching the marshal's face and I could see he didn't believe this last part of what I said. He asked, "How come Mr. Hunnicutt would leave his ranch to a kid he hardly even knew?"

I said, "I figure maybe he didn't want that woman and Mr. Donahue to get their hands on it. Maybe he figured they wouldn't wait for him to die natural as long as they figured the ranch would go to her."

His expression was a little less disbelieving but not very much. He said, "All right, go on."

"Mr. Sligh hid me in a cave. I seen Mr. Donahue and some others following his trail but they went right past where Mr. Sligh had let me off. Soon as they was gone, I lit out. I got a fur piece before some Indians caught me and took me with them."

"What kind of Indians?"

"Cheyennes, I guess. That's what Mr. Sligh said they was.

"They takened me to their village and fed me and gave me some Indian clothes. I stayed about three days. Finally Donahue and Sligh and a bunch of other men rode up. An Indian took me up a gulch. We watched while Donahue and Sligh rode into the village. I reckon them Indians lied and said I wasn't there because Donahue and the others started shooting. They killed a lot of Indians and burned the village down. The Indian with me went back to help out and I went on alone. I found me an old tree at the edge of the gully and I hid under its roots. They went right past. Mr. Hunnicutt's blacksmith seen me but he told Mr. Donahue he didn't."

"Why would he do that?"

"He liked me, and he didn't care much for the goin's on up at the Hunnicutt house."

"What's his name?"

"Ike."

"All right. What happened then?"

"After they left, I came out. I hadn't gone very far, though, before Mr. Sligh caught up with me. He roped me and drug me, and when he stopped that, he beat me up."

"That how you got all them marks?"

"Yes, sir. After that, we come to Denver, and he seen a lawyer named Mr. Rousch about gettin' his hands on the Hunnicutt ranch. They made me sign some papers giving them a share of the Hunnicutt ranch in case I ever got my hands on it. Mr. Sligh locked me in a room. I couldn't jump from the window and I couldn't get out the door. Mr. Sligh come in drunk and passed out, but he was laying on the pocket the key was in so I couldn't get away. Come mornin', though, someone knocked, and Sligh gave me the key and told me to open the door. I did but it wasn't Mr. Rousch. It was Mr. Donahue. Before he knowed what I was up to I ducked out and ran. Mr. Donahue was right behind me but I got away by going out the back. I been hiding ever since, but Donahue's got so many men looking for me I figured my only chance was to find a lawman that wasn't in with them an' tell him the whole story."

The marshal made a low whistle. "That's the damnedest story I ever heard. You got some imagination, kid. What made you think I'd believe a yarn like that?"

I stared at him. All the time I'd been talking, I'd figured he was believing me. Now it looked like he hadn't believed any part of it. He'd hold me here until the Cheyenne sheriff and Donahue showed up and he'd turn me over to them to take back to Cheyenne.

I'd been edging toward the door a little bit at a time. He started toward me and I turned and streaked for it. Trouble was, there was a little bit of sand on the floor and turning so fast made me lose my footing. I sprawled out face down and before I could get up again, the marshal had ahold of me by the back of my Indian deerskin shirt. He lifted me up like I'd been a rabbit or something and he held me there a minute while I tried to claw and kick him, without too much success. He said, "Whoa, you little rooster! Lemme check your story out. What's the name of that hotel you said you an' this Sligh was stayin' at?"

I said, "The Prospector."

"All right." He put me down but he didn't let go of me. He went to the door and called to a man that was passing, "Sam, go over to The Prospector and tell a man named Sligh on the third floor to come over here."

The man nodded and hurried away. The marshal closed the door again. Looked like he knew nigh everybody in town, to be able to put a name to the first man passing by. I quit struggling but he still didn't let go of me. There wasn't no use fighting him. He was too strong for me and too quick. Besides, I figured getting turned over to Sligh was better than getting turned over to Donahue. I'd have a better chance of staying alive long enough to figure something out.

He pushed me into a chair and told me to stay put. He fixed his own chair so it was between me and the door. I couldn't get away and it wasn't no use to try. Pretty soon Sligh come busting in the door. He was scowling and I could see he was feeling mighty sick. He looked at me and said, "So this is where you are, you damn' little whelp!"

The marshal said, "You know this boy?"

Sligh said, "Damn' right I know him! I ought to let you keep him. He's a thief and a liar. What kind of fairy tale did he tell you?"

"Something about inheritin' a big ranch and you tryin' to get it away from him."

Sligh said, "Well, that's a new one. I ain't heard that one before."

He was trying to make me out a regular liar and I wasn't and I didn't mean to sit here without saying anything. I said, "I ain't no liar and everything I've said is true. Ask him how he come to know me."

The marshal said, "How come?"

Sligh's face took on a sorrowful look. "He's my late sister's boy, rest her soul. I takened him to care for like I oughta, but it's been a trial. I swear it's been a trial!"

"How'd he get them Indian duds?"

That one slowed Sligh a bit, but not for long. "Well, he's the runnin' away kind. That's how we come to be here. He run away an' some Cheyennes picked him up an' kep' him until I caught up with him."

"He says you and a man named Donahue attacked the Indian village and killed a lot of Indians."

Sligh shook his head. "More of his lies. The Cheyennes are peaceful now. Soon's they knew he was kin to me they turned him over to me right away."

The marshal glanced at me. He studied me for several minutes before he spoke again. "How'd he get all beat up?"

"Well now, Marshal, I reckon you got me there. I ain't a man of much patience an' I ain't used to young'uns. I kep' tryin' to make him quit runnin' away an' quit lyin' an' I guess I kind of went too far with it." He looked the marshal straight in the eye. "I got me a temper, Marshal. I'm sorry for it sometimes, but I can't rightly he'p it."

That bit of seeming truth telling swayed the marshal more than anything Sligh had said so far. He said, "Suppose I turn him back to you? What you goin' to do?"

"Why, Marshal, I'll do my Christian duty, just like I always have. No kin of mine is goin' to an orphan's home. This boy's a trial, but he's mine an' I'll do the best I can for him."

"He says you had some stolen cattle in your corral."

Sligh looked real sorrowful. "Another of his lies, Marshal. I ain't never takened nothin' that didn't belong to me an' I never will."

"You goin' to beat him again?"

Sligh said, "He's got a beatin' comin', Marshal, an' that's a fact."

The marshal looked at me. "What about it, boy? Think you can do what your uncle tells you to from now on?"

I said, "He ain't my uncle, and he's the liar, not me. Everything he's told you is a damn' big lie!"

Sligh said piously, "Boy, you watch your tongue!"

The marshal said, "All right, Mr. Sligh. Take him along with you. And I wish you luck. Looks to me like you've got a handful raisin' him."

Sligh said, "Thank you, Marshal. Livin' ain't always easy, an' that's a fact."

He looked at me. There was steel in his eyes and a threat that made me hurt in anticipation. He said, "Come on, boy."

I hadn't no choice. I had to go with him. I'd get beat again, but I guessed it was better than gettin' killed by Donahue. I started toward the door and Sligh reached out and grabbed my arm. His fingers bit in so hard it hurt, but I clenched my jaws an' never made a sound.

CHAPTER 13

We never made it to the door. A bunch of horsemen galloped up and hauled their horses to a stop. Dust raised up in the street. Behind the horsemen was a shiny black buggy with yellow wheels. Driving it was Donahue and beside him sat Mr. Hunnicutt's grieving widow, Mrs. Hunnicutt. Sligh tried to yank me on out, maybe thinking he could still get away, but the marshal said, "Hold it, you two. Let's see what's going to happen now."

One of the horsemen, the sheriff, dismounted and tied his horse but all the others kept their seats. Donahue got out of the buggy. He clipped a tether weight to the buggy horse's bridle, then came in with the sheriff. Both looked at me and then at Sligh and then at the big U.S. marshal standing in back of us. The sheriff said, "Howdy, Marshal. I'm John Bidwell, Sheriff of Laramie County, Wyoming Territory."

The marshal nodded. "Pleased to meet you, sheriff. I'm Frank Rittenhouse, U.S. marshal, for this here territory. What can I do for you?"

Bidwell said, "We're lookin' for this boy here. I got a warrant chargin' him with the murder of James Hunnicutt. Appreciate your turnin' him over to us." He produced a paper from his pocket and handed it to Rittenhouse.

The marshal read it laboriously. Or maybe he just

seemed to read it laboriously. Maybe he only wanted time to sort out his thoughts, and to decide what he was going to do. He said, "Hmmm. Seems in order. Suppose you tell me just exactly what this boy here done."

Bidwell turned and faced the window. "Tried to . . . uh . . . attack that lovely lady there, Marshal. That's what he tried to do. Against her will. By force."

Rittenhouse looked out the window at Mrs. Hunnicutt sitting in the buggy clad in black with her eyes cast down. He said, "Hmmm. Looks like the lovely lady might be almost bigger than her attacker, who ain't goin' to weigh much more'n a hundred pounds soakin' wet."

Bidwell looked like a dog with his hackles up. "You questionin' my word, sir?"

Rittenhouse said easily, "Not at all, Sheriff, not at all. It's just that Mrs. Hunnicutt looks pretty capable."

"It's the black, sir. Makes her look bigger than she is."

Rittenhouse nodded. "All right. This here skin-an'-bones boy attacked that lady that looks bigger than she is. I presume he was successful in his attack?"

Bidwell looked even more like a bristling dog. "I beg your pardon, sir! A lady's reputation is at stake!"

Rittenhouse asked, "Did he or didn't he?"

"No sir, he did not! Fortunately for Mrs. Hunnicutt, but unfortunately for her husband, he arrived home at the crucial instant."

"Where did this attack take place?"

"At the Hunnicutt ranch house, sir. In the bedroom usually occupied by Mr. Hunnicutt and his wife."

"All right, Mr. Bidwell. Please go on."

"Mr. Hunnicutt arrived home in time to save Mrs. Hunnicutt from a fate worse than death at the hands of this vicious boy. But the boy was not to be denied. He shot Mr. Hunnicutt in the kitchen of the house."

"So he shot Mr. Hunnicutt. And then what?"

"He leaped upon Mr. Hunnicutt's horse and escaped."

Rittenhouse looked at Donahue. "Who are you?"

Donahue said, "I'm Red Donahue, Mr. Hunnicutt's foreman."

"And you leaped out of your bed in the bunkhouse and ran to the house when you heard the shots? Is that right?"

"Yes sir. That's right."

"Did you take time to dress, Mr. Donahue?"

Donahue looked uncomfortable. "No, I didn't. I just got up out of bed and ran to see what was going on."

"In your underwear?"

"Yes, sir," Donahue growled. "That's how I sleep."

Rittenhouse smiled. "This is interesting. You were in your underwear and according to Jason Ord, he was also in his underwear. Weren't you both afraid of shocking Mrs. Hunnicutt?"

Donahue started to bluster, but Rittenhouse interrupted him. "Never mind. Who reached the house first after hearing the shots, Mr. Donahue? You or one of the members of your crew?"

Donahue looked uncomfortable. "Well, me, I guess."

"I congratulate you. You must react very fast."

"I guess I do." Donahue was scowling now.

Bidwell broke in, "Just what are you gettin' at, Marshal? This here boy was caught in the house by Mr. Donahue. He seen him comin' out. Mrs. Hunnicutt is an eyewitness to the murder of her husband. She can also testify that Jason Ord attacked her."

The marshal glanced out the window. There was at least

a dozen men out there, sitting their fidgeting horses in the street. He asked, "Is that your posse there, Mr. Bidwell?"

"Yes, sir."

"Are they men from Cheyenne, or do they work on the Hunnicutt ranch?"

"Well, they work on the Hunnicutt ranch, I guess."

"But you deputized them all properly?"

"'Course I did. I don't get this, Marshal. You goin' to turn this killer over to us or ain't you? We can get an extradition order if that's what you want."

Rittenhouse said, "Ask Mrs. Hunnicutt to come in. I'd like to talk to her."

"After what she's been through . . ."

Rittenhouse said, "If she can ride in a buggy a hundred and fifty miles, she can come in and talk to me."

"The presence of this vicious boy might frighten her."

Rittenhouse looked him straight in the eye. "Let's see if it does, Mr. Bidwell. Let's see if it does."

Bidwell went out. He went to the buggy and talked to Mrs. Hunnicutt. Then he helped her out of the buggy. She came into the marshal's office clinging to his arm. She looked at me as if she was scared of me. She looked at the marshal and fluttered her eyelids and then looked down at the floor.

Rittenhouse said, "You know this boy, Mrs. Hunnicutt?"

Without looking up and in a voice I could hardly hear she said, "Yes, Marshal."

"Tell me how you happen to know him, Mrs. Hunnicutt."

She looked up appealingly at Donahue. He nodded reassuringly at her. She looked at the floor again and said, "He is Jason Ord. My husband found him wandering across the prairie and brought him home to do the chores."

"What happened on the night your husband was killed?"

"He . . . Jason Ord broke into the house. He . . ."

"*Broke* in? Do you lock the doors?"

"No, sir. I suppose I should have said, came in."

"Where were you, Mrs. Hunnicutt?"

"I was in my room—in the bedroom Mr. Hunnicutt and I shared. I was getting undressed."

"And he just busted in on you?"

"Yes, sir. And attacked me."

"You put up any struggle, Mrs. Hunnicutt?"

Her face turned a dark red. She glanced up and her eyes were murderous. "Of course I did, Marshal. What kind of woman do you think I am?"

"That's what I'm trying to find out, Mrs. Hunnicutt."

Donahue broke in. "We don't have to take this kind of abuse, Mrs. Hunnicutt. Come on. We'll get an extradition order from the judge."

Rittenhouse said, "Do that, Mr. Donahue. I think that would be a good idea."

They all stormed out, slamming the door behind them. I looked at the marshal. "Thanks, Marshal."

"Don't thank me. You ain't out of the woods yet. Not by a long shot. That widow is a mighty good-lookin' woman an' the judge is only human."

I said, "You know I didn't kill Mr. Hunnicutt."

"I don't know nothing of the kind. I don't think you killed him, but thinkin' an' knowin' is two different things."

"What are you going to do?"

"Put you back there in a cell for now. Then we'll sit

back an' see what happens. I don't think them two will even go to the judge."

"What do you think they'll do?"

"I figure they'll try an' bust you out."

He pointed toward the cells and I walked back and into one. He closed and locked the door. It was the first time I'd ever been in jail and I didn't like it much. I felt like a squirrel in a cage. I said, "You going after help?"

"I don't need no help. I can handle Bidwell and Donahue."

He went back into the office. He sat down, put his feet up on the desk and lighted up a long cigar.

I crossed the cell and sat down on the cot. Rittenhouse thought he could handle Bidwell and Donahue and maybe he was right. But it wasn't going to be a case of handling only Bidwell and Donahue. The Hunnicutt ranch was at stake and both Donahue and Mrs. Hunnicutt knew it even if they didn't know about Mr. Hunnicutt's will leaving the place to me. They knew Mrs. Hunnicutt couldn't inherit it if she was convicted of being a part of Mr. Hunnicutt's killing, which she was.

Getting me out and taking me back to Cheyenne and getting me hanged for the murder was the only way Donahue and Mrs. Hunnicutt could get in the clear. They knew it and, having all the Hunnicutt money to draw on, I figure they'd hire whatever help was necessary to get me out of jail. They wouldn't, maybe, want to involve the Hunnicutt crew in a jailbreak, but there were plenty of toughs in Denver that would do it if they was paid for it.

I said, "Marshal?"

"Sure, son. What you want?"

"They'll hire men to bust me out."

"I figure they will, son."

"Hadn't you ought to get some help?"

"Don't need it, son. I can hold this jail. See them shotguns over there?"

I could tell from his tone that there wasn't no use arguing with him. I laid down on the cot and closed my eyes.

I didn't think I would go to sleep, but I did. I guess I felt safer in the marshal's jail than I had any time since Mr. Hunnicutt was killed. When I woke up, it was getting dark outside. The marshal was sitting there, but he wasn't smoking any more. When he saw that I was awake, he asked, "You hungry, son?"

I sat up. "Yes, sir."

"I'll go get us somethin' to eat."

"What about . . . ?"

"Now don't you worry, son. This here jail's built of stone. Them beams on the ceiling is ten inches thick. There's iron bars on all the windows, an' a good lock on the door. Nobody's goin' to get in here whilst I'm gone."

He was so sure, he made me feel better than I had before. He went out and locked the door behind him.

He was gone for what I guessed was half an hour. Then I heard him unlock the door. I guess he stooped to pick up the trays that he'd put down so he could unlock the door and that was all that saved his life. Half a dozen bullets thudded into the door where he'd been standing just a minute before. A couple came into the room and hit the stone wall opposite.

The marshal gave up trying to pick up the trays. He threw himself in through the door, grabbing for his gun as he did. He got across the threshold before the second volley. I heard him grunt as if somebody had hit him in the belly with a fist.

His gun clattered onto the stone floor, still unfired. Men came crowding into the jail. They took his keys off him and came back and unlocked my cell. I'd never seen any of them before, and plainly they didn't belong on any Wyoming ranch. One of them, bearded and sour-smelling, said, "Come on, kid. Don't make no fuss or I'll kick the hell out of you."

There wasn't no use fighting them. I followed the bad-smelling one out into the pitch-black street, stepping over the marshal's body as I did. I didn't know whether he was still alive or not, but I did know it was going to be a long time before he could help me, if he ever could. Donahue had me and whether he killed me outright or arranged to have me hanged, he couldn't afford to let me live for very long.

CHAPTER 14

Well, I didn't know it then, but the marshal was a long ways from being dead. The bullet that had laid him low had only creased his skull, but deep enough to make him bleed a lot. The toughs who rushed the jail saw the blood and the head wound and naturally figured they'd shot him through the head. Rittenhouse finally came to and followed me, prepared to believe everything I'd said, at last, but I didn't know it and I figured it was all over as far as I was concerned.

The men who had broken me out of jail were on foot. The bad-smelling one had a hold on my arm and his fingers bit in like claws. It hurt, but I didn't let him know. I was dragged down the dark street, and around a corner, and a couple of blocks farther and finally around another corner. A buggy loomed up ahead in the dark, and a bunch of men on horses, and the smelly one holding me said, "Here he is, Cap'n."

I knew who he was calling cap'n. Donahue. I also knew that Mrs. Hunnicutt was in the buggy too, because I could smell perfume.

Somebody else took hold of me and the smelly one let go. Some coins clinked and the men who had broken me out of jail disappeared into the darkness. Donahue growled, "Well, you been hard to catch, you little sonofabitch."

I didn't say nothing because there wasn't no use. Donahue asked, "Is the marshal dead?"

I didn't answer, and he cuffed me. "Answer me!"

I said, "They shot him and I guess he's dead. There was a lot of blood."

"Then he won't be coming after us." Donahue lifted me up to one of the men on horseback and climbed into the buggy. The whole outfit fell in behind the buggy, which turned and headed north out of town. Once, a stagecoach passed us in the darkness, its driver yelling at his teams and cracking a long whip, so I figured we was on the stage road to Cheyenne.

I was scared. Nobody was going to help me. They was going to take me to Cheyenne and put me on trial, and there wasn't no chance that I'd be freed. I'd be convicted of murder and sentenced to die.

I guessed I'd have been smarter to stick it out at home, taking the beatings Pa gave me and getting nothing but a hard-scrabble living for my work. But I'd made my choice and now I was going to have to live with it.

We traveled steadily all night. I rode behind one of the men, I didn't know which one. I didn't see or hear the blacksmith, Ike, although I knowed he was along. I thought about him, and remembered that he'd seemed to like me, and for a few minutes I felt a little hope. I talked myself out of it right away. He'd helped me once when I'd been hiding under the tree roots, but he hadn't had to stick his neck out to do it. He wasn't going to stand up for me, not against all these other men.

The sky turned gray in the east and Donahue pulled

off the road into a grove of cottonwoods down along the riverbank. The men all got down and built fires, and they cooked grub that they had in the back of the buggy. The man I'd been riding with gave me a tin plate and told me to help myself. I did, and sat down with my back to a tree and ate. Nobody seemed worried that I would try to escape. They had me and they knew it and so did I.

Finished, I washed my plate in the river by scrubbing it with sand. Then I waited until they would be ready to go again. Mrs. Hunnicutt watched me, a strange expression in her eyes. For all that she'd been carrying on with Mr. Donahue and had caused her husband's death, she didn't seem to be too fond of him. I didn't know much about women then, and still don't, but I figured she was the kind that would never be satisfied with what she had.

We rested the horses for about an hour and a half after we'd finished eating. The men had loosened their saddle cinches and had taken the bits out of their horses' mouths so that they could graze.

The sun came up, and finally we went on again. I saw Ike at the rear of the column. He'd stayed well away from me while we'd stopped to eat and he was still staying away from me. I guessed he figured I'd ask him for help and maybe I would have once. But not now. Not since I'd seen how he tried to keep me from seeing him.

All that day we traveled, stopping every four or five hours to give the horses a little rest. At dark, we pulled off the road again, and built fires and cooked supper. This time the horses got about a three-hour rest before being forced to go on again.

I dozed in the saddle, waking only when I toppled and started to fall out of it. The horses plodded now, refusing to trot or go at any gait other than a walk. Dawn came, and a couple of hours after the sun came up, we rode into Cheyenne.

Donahue and Mrs. Hunnicutt left the others now and headed for the hotel. The other riders went with the sheriff to the jail, a blocky, stone building with bars at the windows and weeds growing out of the thick sod roof.

It was cool inside. The sheriff herded me to one of the cells at the rear and locked me in. He went out with the others, locking the door, leaving me all alone.

Well, I was dead for sleep, and there wasn't no use in me staying awake worrying. I guess a man will fight as long as he figures he's got a chance. I didn't figure I had a chance no more.

I laid down on the cot, which smelled musty and damp. I closed my eyes and for a few minutes my head seemed to whirl, as if the bed and cell and everything was turning around and around. Then I was asleep.

I didn't wake until I heard the door. Even then, I didn't open my eyes, but laid there, breathing regular, pretending I was still asleep.

Sheriff Bidwell had somebody with him. He said, "Come on in and shut the door."

Donahue's voice asked, "What about the kid?"

"He's asleep. But keep your voice down anyway."

"What do you want? Why'd you send for me?"

"That damn Sligh an' Rousch beat us here. They've presented Hunnicutt's will for probate."

"What will, for God's sake?"

"You didn't know about it?"

"No, I didn't know about it. What's it say?"

"Hunnicutt must've scrawled it while he was out

ridin'. It just says he leaves everything to this kid. It also says his wife is a faithless harlot and that he don't want her to have none of it."

"Can he get away with that?"

"Can who get away with what?"

"Hunnicutt. Writin' a will on a scrap of paper that nobody's even witnessed."

"Well, wills are supposed to be witnessed and made out proper, but it'll be easy enough for Sligh an' Rousch to prove it's in the old man's handwritin'. Once they prove that, then the court will likely uphold it."

"But if the kid killed the old man, he ain't supposed to be able to profit by it, is he?"

"What do you mean, *if* he killed the old man? He did, didn't he?"

"Sure he did. I seen him run out of the house with a smokin' gun in his hand."

"Well, all we got to do is prove it, then. If he's sentenced to hang or even to a prison term, they'll vacate the will. And accordin' to Territorial law, the next in line to inherit, even if there ain't no other will, is the widow of the deceased."

I supposed "deceased" meant Hunnicutt. Donahue said, "I'll go see the widow. Maybe we can pull some strings to get the kid's trial set right away. That's a damn' big ranch up there. Its owner ought to have *some* influence in this county."

He went on out. Bidwell sat down at his desk. I could feel him watching me even though my eyes was closed. Finally he said, "No use playin' possum no more."

I opened my eyes. He said, "You ain't got much chance. You know that, don't you, kid?"

I said, "I know it."

"What'd you do it for? After he went an' saved your life an' everything?"

I said, "I didn't do it. Donahue did."

"Sure. Sure. You're innocent. That's what they all say when they're caught."

I said, "What're they payin' you?"

"You watch your tongue, kid. Or by God, I'll beat some respect into you."

I said, "You know what Mrs. Hunnicutt is. It's on that paper Mr. Hunnicutt wrote givin' his ranch to me. You know Donahue is in with her."

"Talk ain't goin' to get you out of this, kid. Mrs. Hunnicutt is a respected member of the community. Donahue is her foreman. You're just a dirty stray. Why the hell should I believe you over them?"

I said, "You shouldn't. I can't give you a goddam thing."

"You watch your tongue, kid!"

I said, "Sure." I was getting kind of mad. I'd been beat and kicked around and hounded and chased like some kind of wild animal. Right now I didn't have one damn' thing to lose so I figured I'd ventilate my feelings by saying whatever come to my mind. I said, "You was in on hiring them toughs in Denver to get me out of jail. How do you think you're going to get out of it when I tell the judge you hired the U.S. marshal killed?"

"I didn't do that. That was Donahue's doin'. An' Mrs. Hunnicutt's."

"You think anybody's going to believe that? You was there."

He got up and came back to the door of my cell. He said, "Kid, you mention that U.S. marshal in court an' I'll beat you so damn' bad you won't ever be able to talk again. I'll bust every tooth in your head and I'll addle your brains so's you'll never make no sense again."

I knew it wasn't no use tryin' to get him on my side. He knowed he was wrong. He knowed Donahue an' Mrs. Hunnicutt had killed Mr. Hunnicutt. But why should he stick up for some dirty stray against two well-known members of the community? Him saying he'd beat me that way put a cold feeling in my belly anyway because I knew he'd do just what he'd said. Memory of the beating Sligh had given me was still fresh enough in my mind so's the thought of another turned me cold.

I looked down at the floor, but I was still mad. Things looked pretty bad for me, but I'd got out of bad spots before and I hadn't given up yet.

I heard the door open behind Bidwell and Sligh and Rousch came in. Rousch said, "We'd like to talk to your prisoner."

Bidwell said, "You got an order from the court?"

"Yes, sir, we got an order from the court." Rousch handed a paper to the sheriff, who read it, scowling. At last he said grudgingly, "All right, talk to him."

Rousch said, "Private."

"Paper don't say that. You talk to him whilst I'm here or not at all."

Sligh and Rousch came back to the bars of my cell. Sligh said, "You little sonofabitch, I ought to let you stew in your own juice."

I said, "But you won't because there ain't no profit in letting me get hung."

Rousch said, "Hold your tongue, boy. We come to help."

"Sure. You don't want me dead until after I inherit that

big ranch. That's the only difference between you and them. They want me dead right now."

Sligh said, "Damn you, when I get my hands on you . . ."

I said, "Some of these days I'm going to grow up. There's going to be some scores to settle when I do."

"You're goin' to hang. Unless me an' Rousch git you out of it."

"How you fixin' to do that?" I said.

"What happened down there in Denver?"

I thought about the threat the sheriff had made about beating me. I didn't know whether he could hear what we was saying or not, but there was a good chance he could. Rousch and Sligh was speaking in whispers but it was a pretty small room. I said, "What do you mean, what happened?"

"Last we heard, you was in the U.S. marshal's custody."

"Well, they got me out."

"The marshal turn you over to them? Just like that?"

I said, "Why don't you ask him?" I knew there hadn't been no witnesses to the shooting of the marshal. Unless I said so, nobody would be able to accuse Donahue and Bidwell of having had a hand in it.

Rousch said, "Hell, the little sonofabitch ain't goin' to help us none."

I wanted to help them because for now they wanted the same thing I did. They wanted me out of here, freed from the murder charge. But with Bidwell listening, I didn't dare say anything that would tie him in with the marshal's death. A couple more beatings like the one Sligh had given me and I wouldn't be no good to anyone, least of all myself.

CHAPTER 15

Well, even though I didn't know it, that bullet had only creased the U.S. marshal's skull. It knocked him cold and gave him a headache that lasted two days. He woke up a couple of hours later and found me gone and right away he decided that all I'd told him must be true. Nobody was going up against a U.S. marshal to bust a ragged stray out of jail unless there was a lot of money to be made from it.

I'd mentioned Cheyenne to him and he knowed Bidwell was Sheriff of Laramie County, so he saddled his horse and headed north as soon as his head had calmed down enough for him to ride.

It's a hundred miles from Denver to Cheyenne, and it took him two days to make it. As soon as he arrived in Cheyenne, he went around from hotel to hotel, asking for Sligh and Rousch. He didn't come to the jail right away, because he knowed the sheriff might make another try for him.

He finally found them and talked to them, and they told him where I was and that I was being held for the murder of Mr. Hunnicutt. Sligh told him he didn't think I had done it. Sligh and Rousch told the marshal they'd help him any way they could.

Mr. Sam Gurd, the U. S. Marshal for Wyoming Territory, was gone up into the northwest corner of the state chasing a stage robber so he wasn't much good to Mr. Rittenhouse. He went to the judge.

The judge told him he didn't have no choice. He had to bring me to trial because there was Mrs. Hunnicutt and Donahue swearing I had killed Mr. Hunnicutt.

Mr. Rittenhouse went back to Sligh and Rousch and told them they had better dig up some kind of proof that I hadn't killed Mr. Hunnicutt. Otherwise, I was going to get convicted of it and hanged. If that happened, I couldn't inherit anything and Sligh and Rousch couldn't share in it unless I did.

Well, they and the marshal took that scrap of paper to the judge and presented it for probate. The judge took the paper and turned it over to the court clerk, after reading it and giving it to the court stenographer to copy in his records.

At least the paper was safe in the custody of the court. Now all Sligh and Rousch and Rittenhouse had to do was prove me innocent. But that wasn't going to be easy. The only two witnesses to what had happened that night, Donahue and Mrs. Hunnicutt, wasn't about to tell the truth. All the rest of the Hunnicutt crew had been asleep until the commotion broke out, so they didn't know but what Mrs. Hunnicutt and Donahue was telling the truth.

After a while, the marshal came to the jail. Sheriff Bidwell must of got quite a shock when he saw him, because he figured he was dead. It was a surprise to me to see him too, the bandage still on his head underneath his hat. The sheriff hung around, listening, until Mr. Rittenhouse turned and said, "Get out of here. I want to talk to this boy alone."

Sheriff Bidwell got red in the face, but he said, "Yes,

sir," and got out of there. He went out front and closed the door behind him. The marshal called, "Stay where I can see you. I don't want you sneaking around and listening at the window."

Bidwell positioned himself in front of the window where we both could see him. The marshal said, "You're in a fix for sure."

I asked, "Does that mean you believe what I said?"

He nodded. "I believe you, but it ain't important what I believe. What counts is what the judge believes. Or the jury. And you ain't got nothing but your own word to back you up."

"Then I guess I'll hang."

He shrugged. "Maybe they won't hang a kid your age, but I wouldn't count on it."

"You don't think I got a chance?"

He shook his head. "Not a chance. Unless you can remember somethin' that would help. Like somebody that might've seen what happened the night Mr. Hunnicutt was killed."

I said, "Everybody was asleep."

He said, "Well, I wish there was somethin' I could do."

I asked, "You going back to Denver now?"

He shook his head. "I got a few days coming to me. Maybe I'll spend it here. I got a little score to settle with them myself." He put a hand up and touched the bandage on his head.

He called to the sheriff and when Bidwell came in, he went on out. I sat down on the cot in my cell. I was getting panicky. If Marshal Rittenhouse thought I didn't have a chance, then I didn't have a chance. I was going to trial and I was going to be convicted and either hung or sent to prison for a long, long time. Nothing was going to change it.

I had to get away. Somehow I had to break out of jail, or break loose when they tried to take me to court. I'd risk getting shot because even getting shot was better than what would happen to me if I didn't get away.

I clenched my fists. My knees was shaking and I felt jumpy all over. I made my voice sound steady. "Sheriff."

"What you want?"

"When's the trial goin' to be?"

He said, "Don't know yet. Mrs. Hunnicutt wants it to be soon. And with the kind of money she's got, she'll likely get her way."

"What do you mean by soon?"

"Tomorrow maybe. Or the day after that."

I asked, "You think I got much chance?"

"Hell, ever'body's got a chance."

"But you don't think that I got much?"

He said, "Mr. Hunnicutt was a well-liked man. No, sir. I don't think you got much chance."

"I didn't do it, Sheriff. Donahue did. I seen him with my own two eyes."

"Sure, kid. Sure. Donahue done it, just like you say. Trouble is provin' that he did."

Later that day, Rittenhouse came back. This time, he didn't bother sending the sheriff out. He said, "Kid, that woman has been spreadin' money around like there wasn't no tomorrow. She's got your trial set for nine o'clock tomorrow mornin'."

I couldn't see that it mattered much. I just stared at him as if I didn't have no hope. I wasn't going to let on but what I'd given up, so maybe they wouldn't be watching me so close. I'd decided the only chance I had was to get away, and I couldn't do that if they suspected me of planning it.

Maybe Marshal Rittenhouse was my friend, I didn't know. What I suspected was that he was here more to settle a personal grudge with Donahue and Mrs. Hunnicutt than to help me out, even though he'd said he believed me now.

Mr. Rittenhouse said, "You look kind of down, kid. You got to keep your dauber up."

I said, "That ain't no use. They're going to hang me sure. I ain't only a kid and I ain't no match for them, with all that money they got and all."

"Maybe the judge won't hang you. Maybe he'll send you to prison instead."

"Sure," I said bitterly. "And I suppose that's better than getting hung. The only difference is that one takes a few minutes an' the other takes the rest of your life."

"No call to be so sour about everything. I come up here to help."

I looked straight at him. "Sure. But help who? If you hadn't got shot down there in Denver, you wouldn't be here and you know it. You don't give a damn for me. You just want to settle your own score for being shot."

He thought about that for a while. "Well, maybe you're right. Maybe I was thinkin' about myself. But there ain't much I can do about your fix."

I said, "I didn't figure there would be."

He studied me for a long, long time. Finally, shaking his head, he went back to where Sheriff Bidwell was. He give the man some money and I heard him say, "See he gets plenty to eat. No damn' jail food. That kid's had a rough time an' it's the least I can do for him."

He was buying off his conscience and I wasn't going to let him get away with it. I yelled, "I don't want no special favors. I'll eat what they got here regular."

Bidwell says, "You heard him. He's a bad one, that kid." He handed the money back to Marshal Rittenhouse. That suited me. I didn't want Mr. Rittenhouse getting away with buying himself out that cheap.

He went out. I laid down on the cot and closed my eyes, pretending I was asleep. It was dark and Bidwell had a lamp burning on his desk when the door opened again.

It was Donahue. He came back to my cell and looked through the bars at me. He said, "Your trial starts tomorrow at nine."

I opened my eyes and looked at him but I didn't say anything. He said, "I want to help you, kid. So does Mrs. Hunnicutt in spite of what you done."

I sat up. "Sure," I said. "You want to help me right up to the gallows."

"Huh uh, kid. I mean it. We can help you if you'll do what I say."

I said, "And what is that?"

"Just confess, that's all. Sign this here paper I brought along. Later on tonight, me an' Mr. Bidwell will see to it you get a chance to get away. There'll be a horse for you, and grub and blankets and whatever else you'll need."

I stared at him. For the first time, hope stirred in me. He wouldn't be here if things was as cut and dried as Mr. Rittenhouse had led me to believe. Donahue was scared or he wouldn't be offering me a chance to escape.

I was tempted, even though I knew what he meant to do once I was outside of the jail. There'd be a horse, all right, but there would also be Donahue waiting out there with a gun. I'd get cut down before I was in the saddle. The whole case would be closed because I would have signed the paper confessing that I'd killed Mr. Hunnicutt. The will Sligh and Rousch had presented for probate would be worthless because you can't inherit nothing from someone you've killed.

I said, "Leave the paper. I'll think on it."

He looked at Sheriff Bidwell. "All right. But don't let the sheriff see."

I said, "Why not? He's in on it."

He looked sad and reproachful. "Son, you think ever'body's against you. An' it just ain't so."

I said, "You just said you an' Mr. Bidwell would see I got a horse."

He shrugged. "All right. He *did* agree to go along with it."

I felt like telling him what a liar I thought he was. Besides being a murderer. He passed the paper through the bars and I walked over and took it. I went back to the cot and sat down again.

I was going to give the paper to Marshal Rittenhouse if he came back. I wasn't going to sign it. Or I didn't think I was.

Then I got to thinking. Maybe getting shot wasn't so bad when I faced up to what was going to happen if I went to trial. Shooting was better than hanging any day. Maybe it was better than spending the rest of your life in prison, knowing all the time you didn't do what you was in there for.

I pushed the paper under the mattress. I just couldn't decide what to do.

CHAPTER 16

I didn't sleep too good that night. I kept thinking about the paper under the mattress, and the offer Mr. Donahue had made. Maybe if I signed the paper and got away, I could outwit Mr. Donahue and keep from getting shot. There wasn't much chance but there *was* a chance.

But I wasn't going to do it yet. My trial began tomorrow at nine, and I figured I'd go through a day of it just to see how bad things looked. If they looked bad enough I'd have to take Mr. Donahue's offer and then try to get out of it alive if I could.

Sheriff Bidwell brought my breakfast to me at seven. It was a big breakfast of eggs and steak and biscuits and honey and I ate like a condemned man, which I guess I was. I said, "What you trying to do, buy off your conscience for the price of a meal?"

He said, "You're a nasty little sonofabitch. If you was allowed to grow up, you'd be a bad one. Good thing you ain't goin' to get that chance."

I could see there wasn't no use talking to him. He knowed he was in the wrong. But, people bein' what they are, he was trying to square his own conscience by convincing himself I was the one that was in the wrong. He probably had himself half convinced I really had shot Mr.

Hunnicutt, or at least that there was enough doubt to make the supposition reasonable.

He didn't give me no water to clean up with, and I had no chance to clean up my clothes. I figured they wanted me to look dirty and disreputable when I appeared in court. Wasn't no mirrors to look into, but I knowed I was dirty, with several weeks' fuzz on my face, an' them dirty, greasy, ragged Indian clothes. I'd finished and had been layin' on the cot for a while when he said, "Come on, kid. It's time."

I got up and he unlocked my cell. I went out, with him following, a double-barreled shotgun in his hands. He wasn't taking no chances with me, or maybe he just wanted to impress the judge and jury with what a dangerous character I was.

We went out of the jail and walked to the courthouse. He could of put handcuffs on me, but he likely figured that wouldn't look as good as this.

There was a big crowd gathered in front of the courthouse and they looked at me like I was some kind of wild animal. The little girls hid behind their mothers' skirts, an' the men scowled, an' the women looked like they would if somebody had led a wolf in amongst them. I thought that these was the same people that would be on the jury, and by God, they already had their minds made up about me.

Sheriff Bidwell herded me inside. We sat down front, and once he had me in there, he handcuffed me to the bench. The courtroom filled up as soon as they opened the doors for the people. I didn't have no lawyer, but that didn't surprise me none. After a while, though, a real young, nervous man came in and he sat down by me and said, "Kid, I'm your court-appointed lawyer. I'm supposed to defend you. You want to plead guilty?"

I said, "Does that mean I'm sayin' I done it?"

"That's what it means. If you plead guilty an' throw yourself on the mercy of the court, maybe you'll get off with life imprisonment. That means you could get out in twenty years if you behave yourself."

I said, "I didn't do it. Mr. Donahue did. Him an' Mrs. Hunnicutt."

He said, "Lyin' ain't going to help you none."

I said, "You supposed to stick up for me or just make it easier for them to get me hanged?"

He said, "That attitude ain't going to get you nowheres, son. But I'll do what I can for you all the same."

I thought, Sure. You do what you can to get me sent to prison.

Pretty soon the judge came in, wearing long black robes, and somebody said, "All rise. The District Court of the County of Laramie, Territory of Wyoming, is now in session. Judge William J. Whitaker presiding."

Everybody got up, including me and my "lawyer," and the judge settled himself behind the bench. He was a skinny, scraggly looking man with eyes as hard as marbles and a mouth so thin you'd of sworn there wasn't no lips at all. His forehead was high an' bony an' his cheeks hollow. His nose was pointed, and hooked like the beak of a hawk. I wasn't going to get no sympathy out of him, or even fair treatment. Like all the rest of the people hereabouts, he just wanted me swept under the rug and the sooner the better for everybody.

He said, "Clerk, read the charge."

The clerk got up. He had a paper in his hand. He said,

"People versus Jason Ord, charged in the murder of James Hunnicutt of this county." He gave the date Mr. Hunnicutt had been killed.

The judge asked, "Is the defendant represented by counsel?"

My "lawyer" got up and said I was. The judge said, "Will the prosecutor proceed?"

Another man got up. He started talking about all he was goin' to prove—that I was a depraved and unregenerate runaway who had been befriended by Mr. Hunnicutt and had repaid that friendship by turning on his benefactor. I had forced my attentions on Mrs. Hunnicutt, he said, and, when caught in the act, had shot and killed my benefactor, stolen his horse and run away.

First of all, he called Mr. Donahue to the stand. Donahue went up, not looking at me. He raised one hand and put the other on the Bible and swore he would tell the truth. The prosecutor asked him his name and what he did for a living and when all that was over, he asked, "What happened on the night of June 28th, Mr. Donahue. Just tell us in your own words, if you please."

Donahue said, "I'd got up to go to the outhouse, sir. I was only wearin' my underwear."

A little laugh went through the courtroom, like there was somethin' funny about goin' to the outhouse in your underwear.

The prosecutor said, "Go on, Mr. Donahue."

"Well, I heard Mrs. Hunnicutt screamin' up at the house. Right then I seen Mr. Hunnicutt ride in. He jumped off without even botherin' to tie his horse. He busted into the house."

"And then what, Mr. Donahue?"

"Well, I stood there a minute, tryin' to figure out what I ought to do. I didn't have nothin' on but my underwear an' I figured it wouldn't be decent for me to go up there an' let Mrs. Hunnicutt see me like that."

I thought sourly that she had seen him with a lot less on, but the prosecutor said, "What did you do, Mr. Donahue?"

"I headed back into the bunkhouse to put on my pants, but right then I heard a shot. I ran for the house, without takin' time for the pants, an' when I got to the kitchen window, I seen Mr. Hunnicutt lyin' on the floor with blood all over him."

"What else did you see, Mr. Donahue?"

"That kid there, with a smokin' pistol in his hand. An' Mrs. Donahue, cryin' an' carryin' on an' the nightclothes purty near ripped off of her."

I looked over at Mrs. Hunnicutt. She was dabbing at her eyes with a little scrap of a handkerchief, and her face was as white as a sheet. A murmur went through the courtroom, a murmur of sympathy for the poor bereaved woman and I knowed right then for sure that I wasn't going to get out of this. I looked over at the jury. Half a dozen of them was looking at me an' if looks could kill, I'd have been dead right then.

I was going to have to sign the confession for Donahue and try to keep him from killing me when I tried to get away. There wasn't no other choice. I could tell I was finished if I waited for the jury and the judge to decide what ought to be done with me. Maybe they wouldn't hang me on account of I was still a kid, but they'd sure as hell send me to prison for the rest of my life.

The prosecutor said, "Then what, Mr. Donahue?"

"Well, this kid ran out. I tried to grab him, but he got away from me an' jumped on Mr. Hunnicutt's horse. He lit out like the devil was after him an' I yelled for the crew to get up and saddle horses to go after him."

"Then what did you do, Mr. Donahue?"

"Well, sir, I tried to calm Mrs. Hunnicutt as best I could."

I thought, Sure you did. In your underwear. But I didn't say anything. It wouldn't of done me any good.

As if the case against me needed clinching, the prosecutor said, "That's all, Mr. Donahue." He looked at the judge while Donahue was leaving the stand. He said, "I call Mrs. Hunnicutt."

She got up. She was dressed in black, with some white lace at her throat and at the cuffs. She looked like a grieving widow, but that black dress was tight in just the right places to show that she was a damn' good-looking woman with lots of all the things women is supposed to have. Once more a murmur of sympathy went through the courtroom. She walked to the witness stand, dabbing delicately at her eyes with that tiny scrap of lace handkerchief, and when she got almost there, the prosecutor took her arm and helped her until she had sat down and settled herself.

He said, "I'm deeply sorry to have to put you through this, Mrs. Hunnicutt, and I'll be as brief as possible."

Her voice was almost a whisper, but I heard it. "Thank you, sir."

For a minute I forgot about myself and the trouble I was in and thought about Mr. Hunnicutt, who'd caught this "grieving" widow in bed with another man and had got hisself killed by the other man. It made me mad. They were going to get away with it and I was damned if I could see how I could stop them.

The prosecutor said in a voice that dripped sympathy, "Please tell us what happened on the night of June 28th, Mrs. Hunnicutt."

She looked across at me and I don't know how she did it but her face got even whiter than it had been before. She said, "Mr. Hunnicutt was gone. He was often gone."

Again that murmur of sympathy.

She said, "I was asleep. Suddenly . . ." She stopped again as if she was unable to go on. The prosecutor said, "I know this is painful, Mrs. Hunnicutt, but please go on."

"Yes, sir. That young man burst into my room in his underwear. He was like a wild man. He ripped at my clothes, and he struck me, sir. I fought, but I was no match for him."

I stared at her. She weighed twenty pounds more than I did and it seemed like somebody would notice that but nobody did.

The prosecutor said sympathetically, "Please go on, Mrs. Hunnicutt."

I looked at the jury and at the people crowded into the courtroom. It was like they was under some kind of spell. Their eyes was bright an' they kep' lickin' their lips, an' they couldn't take their eyes off Mrs. Hunnicutt. She managed to turn a deep red an' she said, "I can't go on, sir, not in front of all these people."

"All right, Mrs. Hunnicutt. I think we all know what he tried to do. Please tell us what happened then."

"I heard a horse gallop up to the house. I heard the door

and I heard footsteps on the stairs. My husband burst into the room, a gun in his hand."

"And then?" Most of the crowd looked disappointed that the prosecutor hadn't made her go into the details of what I was supposed to have done.

"They struggled. They fought all the way down the stairs and into the kitchen. I followed, on the chance that I'd be able to help."

I thought, Sure. Help Donahue.

"And then?"

"They reached the kitchen. That young man must have gotten the gun away from my husband. I heard the shot, and my husband fell to the floor."

"What did the defendant do?"

"He ran, sir. He ran. He stole my husband's horse and rode away into the night."

"Thank you, Mrs. Hunnicutt." He looked at my lawyer and said, "Cross-examine?"

My lawyer got up. "I have no questions, your honor."

I whispered, "She lied! Make her admit she lied!"

The judge pounded on his desk. He said, "Counselor, you will instruct your client that he is not to speak unless he is on the stand."

"Yes, your honor."

Everybody was scowling at me. Even if I hadn't been entirely sure of it before, I was now. I was a dead duck. Unless I could get away.

The court recessed for noon, and after the crowd had cleared, the sheriff picked up his shotgun and herded me out again.

There was a crowd in front of the courthouse to watch me when I came out. And suddenly I knowed this was the best chance I was ever going to get. The street was full of people and the sheriff couldn't fire his scattergun for fear of hitting one of them. Unless one of the surprised townsmen reached out and grabbed me, I had a chance to get away.

At the foot of the courthouse steps, I bolted. I knocked a woman down and she screamed, and behind me I heard Sheriff Bidwell and some others yell, "Stop him! Stop the little sonofabitch!"

Hands reached for me, but I managed to tear away. I went through the crowd and finally I was in the clear. The shotgun blasted behind me, once, twice, but I knowed it was pointed at the sky. I ran like a rabbit between two buildings, scattering old tin cans with an awful clatter.

But I was loose, and I wasn't dead. How I'd stay that way, I didn't know, but I sure did mean to try.

CHAPTER 17

I don't know what had happened to Sheriff Bidwell. He was probably hemmed in by the milling crowd and unable to get right after me. Donahue wasn't even in the street. I suppose he was confident I would be convicted and had never given the possibility that I might escape any thought. The crowd itself was too surprised to pursue me immediately. But one man there in the street wasted no time in seizing his opportunity. That man was Sligh.

I reached the end of the passageway and sprawled headlong when I tripped over a pile of trash. Scratched but otherwise unhurt, I scrambled to my feet and went on, throwing a quick backward glance over my shoulder.

There was a man's figure in the passageway, outlined against the light at the other end. I didn't recognize him then, supposing he was only the first of many that would be hunting me throughout the town.

I turned right, running like a deer. My pursuer jumped over the pile of trash that had brought me down. Longer legged, he commenced to gain on me as I ran down the narrow alley. Looking back once more as I neared the end of it, I recognized him, Sligh.

Right now, I knowed, I needed him. And he needed me. Time enough later to worry about getting away from him. For the moment our interests was the same. He didn't want me convicted of murder no more than I wanted to be. He didn't want me caught. He was evil and greedy and I didn't mean nothing to him, but right now I could use all the help that I could get. I stopped, panting and sweating and let him catch up with me. He said, "Come on," and ran ahead of me, trotting now.

Cutting mostly across vacant lots but steadily heading toward the edge of town, he led me along until finally he judged, I guess, that he had left the crowds behind. Soon enough there'd be mounted, armed posses scouring Cheyenne, but maybe by then we would be gone.

There was a run-down livery barn on a street near the railroad depot, and he told me to wait whilst he went inside. I snuck up to the door to watch and I seen him hit the stableman with a gunbarrel. The man crumpled to the ground without a sound.

Sligh went back among the stalls, carefully selecting horses for us to ride. He passed up four before he picked one he liked, and he passed up three more before he found another one. Leading the two haltered animals, he came toward the front of the livery barn.

I went in. There was blood on the liveryman's head and I wondered if he was dead. I took one of the horses and bridled and saddled him with stuff Sligh threw out of the little tackroom toward the front. He went to the door and looked out before he swung to his horse's back. I followed suit. He said, "Come on. Keep up."

He didn't need to worry about that. I had no intention of falling behind. Without Sligh I wouldn't have no chance of getting out of Cheyenne without being caught and I knowed getting away from him would be a lot easier than getting away from half a dozen posses who, by now, must be scouring the town.

He cut left through a vacant lot, crossed the tracks and dropped down into a gully where we'd be out of sight. He held his horse to a trot. He kept looking behind for pursuit and so did I, but nobody appeared. After we'd gone a mile, he climbed his horse out of the gully and rode behind a low hill. Here, he stopped. He said, "Looks like we made it, kid. For now at least."

I asked, "What are we goin' to do?"

"We'll decide that later. Right now the main thing is to keep you from gettin' caught."

For now we wanted the same thing. But I wasn't stupid. I'd given Sligh a lot of trouble and sooner or later he'd beat me and maybe drag me the way he had once before. He had a gleam in his eyes and I didn't like the way he was looking at me.

The truth was that Sligh liked hurting things, whether it be dogs, horses, calves, or people. I made up my mind that I'd use him by letting him get me safely away from Cheyenne. But if he tried to beat me, I wasn't going to let him get away with it.

Sligh was stronger than me, but I had an advantage I hadn't used before. I was small and I was quick.

We rode steadily all afternoon. Sligh knew exactly how hard to push the horses so that he got the most out of them without wearing them out or killing them. Every few hours we'd stop, and unsaddle, and cool the horses' backs. We let them drink sparingly at every stream we crossed. If they wanted to crop a mouthful of grass along the way, we let them. If we saved their strength and rested them occasionally, they'd travel all day and all night and that would put us farther ahead of the pursuit than running them until they were plumb wore out.

At nightfall we stopped once more to rest them. We didn't have nothing to eat, but we drank some water from the stream. We both laid down. Sligh didn't close his eyes, figuring maybe I'd try to get away, which I sure would have if he'd gone to sleep. Seeing he wasn't going to sleep, I closed my eyes and did. It was dark when he woke me up.

We mounted and rode out again. Sligh wasn't headed south. He was headed west and little south, toward the high Colorado mountains. I had no way of knowing what was in his mind. Maybe he just meant for both of us to hide out until the chase died down. Maybe he had some other plan.

All night we rode, pretty much letting the horses pick their own way, their eyesight being a lot better than ours. All Sligh done was to hold them to a certain direction.

I was pretty doggoned cold. I didn't have no coat, nor blankets neither. I shivered most of the night, my teeth sometimes chattering. I sure was glad to see the line of gray along the eastern horizon, and even gladder to see the bright rim of the sun poke its way into sight.

Sligh stopped a little while after that. He kept looking at me and I knowed the beating was coming now. I got off my horse, looking around for something I could fight back with. There was a round, smooth rock about the size of both my fists right at my feet, and, hidden by my horse's body, I stooped and picked it up.

I held the rock behind me as I looked over my horse's back at Sligh. He got down from his own horse, looking toward me. He said, "You little sonofabitch, you sure do try a man."

I said, "I'm sorry, Mr. Sligh."

"Sorry ain't enough, kid. I think it's time somebody teached you to do what your elders tell you to."

I said, "Yes, sir. I'm sorry, sir." I couldn't loosen the horse's saddle without letting the rock in my hand show. One rock only gave me one chance. If I missed with it, I knew what the price would be. He wouldn't kill me, but he'd come close. Even closer than he had last time. It might be months before I'd heal. I might never completely heal. So I had to let him get close to me and I had to take my time and do it right when I did throw the rock.

He had loosened his horse's saddle and had takened the bit out of the horse's mouth so that he could graze. He came around his horse and said, "Come on, kid. Loosen the cinch."

I said, "Yes, sir," and pretended to be working on the cinch. He came around the rump of my horse, eyes on what my hands were doing, meaning to let me finish before he grabbed hold of me.

He was less than four feet away. He wasn't looking straight at me but at my hand, tugging on the latigo preparatory to loosening the cinch.

I let go of it. I drew back the rock, which was round and smooth. He glanced up in time to see what I was doing, but he didn't duck. He lunged for me.

It was now or never. Wordlessly I prayed to God that I could throw straight and hard enough.

I let go the rock. There was only three feet for it to travel, and it went straight and true. The sound as it struck Sligh on the forehead was mighty plain.

I pulled away from his outstretched, grasping hands, and ran. I hadn't hit him hard enough, I thought. And now, because I had hurt him, the beating would be even worse than if I'd taken it without fighting back.

I ran about a hundred feet. I didn't hear him chasing me and turned my head to look.

Sligh was on the ground behind the horse. Stunned, I thought, and laying there playing possum waiting for me to come back. I stopped and stared at him for as long as I dared. Maybe he really *was* unconscious, I thought. Maybe he wasn't only stunned. If that was true, I had better do something before he came to again.

Cautiously I returned. He didn't move. I couldn't even see him breathe. I approached keeping my horse between us so that if he did lunge for me, I'd have a chance of getting away. I took the horse's reins and pulled him away. Passing Sligh's horse, I grabbed his reins too and led both horses away about fifty feet.

I had both horses and I could run for it. But Sligh still had a gun and the gun would make it possible for him to shoot me as I mounted or at least to get another horse. A step at a time, I walked toward him, never letting my eyes stray from his face. I'd see it if he gathered his muscles to move, I thought.

There was blood on his forehead where the rock had struck, and a big lump was already forming there. His eyes were closed.

He laid on his side, the gun and holster under him. I circled him, my eyes now on the walnut grips of the gun. I'd be easy prey for him when I stooped to take the gun.

The rock I had hit him with lay about half a dozen feet away. I picked it up. With it poised to strike again if need be, I stooped and put my hand on the grip of his gun.

It stuck in the holster. For an instant I took my eyes off

Sligh's face. I yanked on the gun and it came free, but at that instant Sligh moved like a mountain lion.

Blindly I swung with the rock, and it hit him a grazing blow just behind the ear. Stunned, he settled back long enough for me to leap away, to come to my feet and to cock the gun. I shrilled, "Don't you come after me! I'll kill you. I swear I will."

The gun muzzle was waving around and I was shaking all over as if I had a chill. Maybe that was what stopped him. He knew the gun could and would go off with the slightest pressure on the trigger. He knew it might even go off accidentally even if he didn't move toward me. There was a good chance the bullet would miss but he didn't want to count on it. He said soothingly, "Easy, kid. Easy. I won't lay a hand on you. I promise it."

I said, "Sure. You promise. But once you git this gun away from me your promise won't be worth a hoot."

I backed off. When I was thirty or forty feet away I raised the gun to eye level, sighting it on him. The farther I got from him the steadier I got. I reached the horses.

I'd have to move fast now, I thought. I had to shove the gun in my belt, grab the reins of one horse and mount the other before he could reach me on foot. It wouldn't be easy, because he'd be running as he'd never run before.

Still pointing the gun at him, I got my own horse's reins arranged. Leaving him, I got the other horse's reins and tied them and then looped them around the saddle horn. While I did, I held the cocked revolver against my body with my arm. Once he started to come at me, but I dropped the reins and pointed the gun at him again and he stopped.

Finally I was ready. I said, "Back off. Back off or I'll shoot."

I guess he figured the odds on me hitting him weren't too good at this distance because he said, "Hell with you, kid."

He wasn't going to move, and the instant I shoved the gun into my belt, he'd make a run for me. I got behind my horse and suddenly jammed the revolver into my belt, first letting the hammer ease down.

I jammed a foot at the stirrup and my heart sank clear down into my belly as it missed. I jabbed at the stirrup with it a second time, and this time made it. I swung to the horse's back and kicked him in the ribs, at the same time letting loose with a high, shrill yell.

The horse jumped and for a breathless minute I thought he was going to buck. He took a long jump. The tied reins pulled taut and I thought, "Oh God, what if they break?"

Sligh was there, and he grabbed my horse's headstall, and I kicked out at him without even thinking. My foot, moccasin clad, hit his head, and the horse jumped again at the same time, and he staggered back, but recovered quickly enough to grab at the second horse as he passed.

Frightened, this one swung his hind end around and lashed out with both hind feet at Sligh. One hoof caught him in the thigh and he went to the ground, writhing and cursing helplessly with pain.

But I was away. With both horses and Sligh's gun, I was free again. I didn't give a damn no more about getting cleared of killing Mr. Hunnicutt. I didn't give a damn about Mr. Hunnicutt's big ranch. All I wanted to do was stay alive. And free.

CHAPTER 18

I looked back from the top of a little knoll about half a mile from where I'd left Mr. Sligh. He was just standing there looking after me, but I could imagine what he was saying, or if he wasn't saying anything, what his thoughts was.

I went down the slope and he was lost to sight and I hoped I would never see him again.

What I had to do, I thought, was to get clear out of Wyoming just as fast as I could. I'd go west, I thought, all the way to California. Only when I had put a thousand miles between myself and those chasing me could I feel safe again.

But getting to California wasn't going to be as easy as saying it. In the first place, I was riding a stolen horse and leading a second one. There was telegraph lines out of Cheyenne to points west, and as soon as Sligh got back to Cheyenne I could count on the word going out to law officers for five hundred miles around.

I thought about all the charges against me. Attempted rape, for a starter. Murder. Horse stealing. Jail break. Escape from custody. Assault. If you'd listen to the charges, you'd of thought I was a real desperate character. Only to my way of thinkin', I hadn't done nothin' but try and keep from going to prison for something I hadn't done.

I wondered how long it would take Sligh to find a ranch where he could get a horse. He didn't have no gun and it wasn't likely he had enough money on him to buy a horse outright. But if I knew Mr. Sligh, he'd figure some way of getting one.

I headed west. For a while I loped the horses but when it got hot and they began to sweat, I eased up and let them walk a while. Soon as they'd cooled, I loped them again.

There ain't nothing emptier than Wyoming territory. You can ride half a day and never see a cow. You can travel for days without seeing no ranch houses. But this day I was lucky, I guess. All of a sudden, I come over a little hill and there ahead of me was a house.

It wasn't much of a house, that was sure. It had been built out of blocks of sod cut right out of the ground and laid up like bricks. They'd have to of gone a long ways to get them, but they had stout logs laying across the sod walls to make a roof and on top of the logs they'd laid more sod and dirt until maybe the roof was two feet thick. The dirt roof wouldn't shed water but it would soak it up, and there ain't many rains in Wyoming that will soak through two feet of dirt.

I stopped as soon as I seen the house. I sat there looking down. Out behind the place there was a little corral made out of crooked poles that was likely the branches of cottonwoods. There was one horse in the corral. There was a shed behind the house, and a root cellar, and three white chickens scratchin' in the yard.

Well, I knew Mr. Sligh would follow my trail, most probably, an' if he did, he'd come on this place before the day was out, even travelin' afoot. He'd get that horse and then he could really come after me. He might even get a gun down there.

I had to do him out of that horse. I didn't have no choice. So I rode down toward the house, keeping my hand fairly close to the grips of Sligh's gun, which I had stuffed into my belt.

The chickens didn't pay me no mind, but the horse raised his head and stared at me. And then, out of the house, a girl came, carrying a shotgun in her hands. She looked to be about as old as me. She had yellow hair and a homespun dress that was gettin' too small for her and showed that she was goin' on a woman in spite of her being only about sixteen.

I said, "Howdy, ma'am."

She said, "I ain't no ma'am. Even you can see that plain enough."

I said, "Sure. I can see."

She said, "What you want?"

I said, "I'm bein' chased. I got to turn that horse out of your corral so's the man chasin' me can't get his hands on it."

"What's he chasin' you for?"

I said, "It's a long story and you wouldn't believe it no way."

She stared at me without saying nothing for a long, long time. At last she said, "I might. I got coffee on, an' there's some side meat an' biscuits left over from Pa's breakfast. You can have 'em if you're a mind."

Well, I didn't figure stoppin' a few minutes would hurt and besides she had that shotgun and just might use it if I tried to turn her horse out of the corral. I'd caught a whiff of the side meat and all of a sudden I was hungry as could be.

I got down off my horse and I tied the two of them to one of the corral poles. I said, "I'm obliged, ma' . . ." I stopped. I said, "What you want me to call you if I don't call you ma'am?"

"Name's Jessie. You can call me that."

I said, "Sure, Jessie. My name's Jason."

She looked like maybe she was sorry she'd asked me to eat. She went in, not putting the shotgun down. I said, "You can't get stuff off the stove 'less you put down that gun."

"I guess not." She put it down beside the stove.

I asked, "Is it loaded?"

"Sure it's loaded. What do you think?"

I knew she was lying by the way she said it. I sat down at the rough plank table and she poured me a tin cup of hot coffee that sure tasted good. She brought me a plate of crisp side meat and half a dozen biscuits, along with a pot of jam. She asked, "Why you being chased?" She sat down across from me and watched me whilst I ate.

All of a sudden I wanted to tell somebody. I said, "I'm supposed to have killed a man named Mr. Hunnicutt. I'm supposed to have attacked his wife and killed him when he caught me doin' it."

For a minute she looked scared. I said, "See. You believe it too."

She said firmly, "I do not. Not yet anyway. Not until I hear your side of it."

I said, "I ran away from home because Pa was always beating me. I got out here in Wyoming and my horse up and died and I figured I was a goner for sure. This Mr.

Hunnicutt found me and took me home with him and give me a job. I wouldn't kill him and I wouldn't have nothing to do with his wife."

"Well, who did do it then?"

"His foreman. Man named Red Donahue. I just happened to get up to . . . well, go to the outhouse, and I heard Mr. Hunnicutt come galloping in. Little later, I heard a shot. I went to look and they heard me, and I knowed they'd kill me if they could. So I jumped on Mr. Hunnicutt's horse and got away."

"Then what?" Her eyes was about as big as saucers.

"I come to a little shack. There was a man there named Sligh. He put a gun on me and looked in the saddlebags and he found a paper signed by Mr. Hunnicutt leaving his whole big ranch to me."

She looked like she didn't believe me. I said, "You don't believe me."

She lied, "Sure I do. What happened then?"

"Well, he helped me to get away. He hid me in a cave. But soon's Donahue give up, he come and caught me and he beat the hell out of me."

I looked at her. I said, "Damn it, either you believe me or not and I don't much care which. I'm going to turn that horse out of the corral and there ain't no use picking up that shotgun again because I know it ain't loaded and so do you."

She looked straight at me for a long, long time. Her eyes was clear and blue and they seemed to look right down into the middle of me like I couldn't hide nothing from her if I tried. She said finally, "I believe you, Jason."

"You going to turn that horse out, like I said?"

She said, "I'm goin' to do better than that. I'm goin' to

turn him out, an' I'm goin' to take your two horses an' ride to where Pa is. This Sligh will think you ate here an' went on, an' he'll follow trail. I'll get Pa an' we'll come back an' see what we can do about gittin' you away."

I didn't know whether to believe her or not. If she was lying about believin' me, she'd leave me here afoot whilst she went after her pa, who would go after the sheriff, who would catch me and throw me in jail again.

But she'd believed me, or I thought she had, and I guessed it wouldn't hurt none to believe her. I was in a fix anyhow, and not likely to get out of the country unless I had some help.

I was all done eating and she said, "You come on with me. I got me a hidey place that I used to go to when I was little."

She went out. She led me out across the prairie for almost a quarter mile and finally she come to a place where the dirt was hollowed out from under a brushy little bank. It wasn't no bigger than I could barely squeeze into but I knowed nobody would pay it no mind unless they knowed a hiding place was here. She said, "You stay here an' don't come out. Let's see if this Mr. Sligh won't just go on by."

I crawled under the overhang. She went away and I sat for a while thinking I was a poor damn' fool for trusting her when I hadn't met her only about an hour before. Then I remembered them clear blue eyes and the way she seemed to look right into me and I reckoned she'd do what she said she would.

I was tired, so I laid back and closed my eyes. When I woke it was late afternoon and somebody was yelling down there at the sod house.

I raised up and peeked and sure enough it was Sligh. He went into the house, and was gone a while, and when he came out he was eating and stuffing things into his pockets. Food I figured. He hadn't bothered with the shotgun because he'd likely checked it and found no load in it.

He yelled, "Kid, you come on out! I ain't gonna beat you! You trust old Sligh an' we'll both be livin' in that big house at Hunnicutt's."

He went and poked into the root cellar and he looked around, puzzled like for a long time. Then, like a hound, he made a circle of the place until he picked up the tracks of the two horses leaving there. He fooled around for a minute over the tracks of the horse that had been in the corral. I guess he could tell pretty quick that the horse hadn't had a rider, because he give up on him.

Walking, then, he left, following the trail Jessie had left as she rode my horse away and led the other one.

I laid back under the overhang. I didn't know what to think of Jessie, but I was willing to bet her pa wasn't going to believe me as quick as she had. I wasn't out of the woods yet, not by a long shot.

But every minute I was free was a minute I didn't have to spend in jail. The sky was blue and the sun was warm and there was somebody, at least, that believed what I had said. I was learning to be glad for little things, like being alive, and being free, and having my belly full, and having time to rest.

I figured sooner or later, Sheriff Bidwell and Donahue would be along. I didn't know whether they'd be fooled by the ruse or not.

They'd find Jessie and her pa. They'd find the horses

and they'd know she had fooled them in order to protect me.

There wasn't no place you could hide on this Wyoming prairie for very long. I'd better enjoy being free whilst I could.

CHAPTER 19

It wasn't long after Sligh had left, afoot, that two more horsemen came riding in. They was following trail too and they hailed the house, getting no more answer than Sligh had got. It was easy enough to recognize them two. They was Mr. Donahue and Sheriff Bidwell. They'd picked up our trail, probably because the stable owner had complained to the sheriff about the two horses Sligh had stolen from him. They poked around a while, then finally made a big circle of the place. They picked up the trail of the two stolen horses, and of Sligh, afoot, following. They lined out the same way Sligh had and disappeared.

I settled back and closed my eyes. It sure would be nice, I thought, to live out here with no more to do than that girl Jessie had to do and not have nobody chasing you. I hadn't been daydreaming more'n about half an hour when I heard somebody else yellin' down there at the sod house. I poked my head up and recognized the U.S. marshal from Denver, Mr. Rittenhouse. All the goin's on hadn't fooled him none. He'd seen Sligh's tracks and mine and he'd seen Donahue's tracks and those of the sheriff, and he'd seen them little footprints left by Jessie and he'd added two and two and come out four.

He shouted, "Hey, Jason! I know you're there. You come on out now, you hear?"

I laid back and didn't make no sound. The marshal yelled, "Jason, I been talkin' to some of the Hunnicutt crew. I talked to the blacksmith, Ike. He says you didn't kill Mr. Hunnicutt. He says it was Donahue an' that woman did it when they got caught by Mr. Hunnicutt."

I figured maybe he was just trying to get me to come out so I didn't move.

He yelled, "Jason, you better let somebody try and help you. You ain't going to make it unless you do. Turn yourself over to me and I'll see you get a decent trial. I'll get them crew members at Hunnicutt's to come in and tell what they know."

Well, I just didn't know what to do. Jessie had stuck her neck way out by helping me and maybe by now she'd talked her pa into helping me too. Sligh would likely kill anybody that got in his way, he was that desperate. So was Mr. Donahue. Sheriff Bidwell was likely to do whatever Donahue told him to, figuring Donahue was going to end up owning the Hunnicutt ranch and be a big power in the county.

Marshal Rittenhouse yelled, "Jason, you think on it. I can find you if I'm a mind to, but I'd rather you come out on your own!"

I thought about it two or three minutes. I knowed if I stayed hid here I was going to get found sooner or later. If Sligh found me, he'd get even with me for hitting him with a rock. If Donahue and Bidwell found me, I'd end up dead before I ever got to Cheyenne.

I crawled out of my hiding place and stood up. Marshal Rittenhouse yelled, "Come on down, boy. You are doing the right thing."

I walked on down to the sod shack. I said, "I sure hope you ain't lying to me."

"I ain't, boy. 'Course, I can't guarantee the judge will let you go but I think he will. I talked to three or four of Hunnicutt's crew besides that blacksmith Ike and they all say the same thing."

I said, "There was a girl here when I rode in. She fed me and believed me and she hid me out. I'd ought to leave a note for her."

"All right. Let's go in and see if there's any paper to write it on."

We went into the sod shack. There wasn't no paper I could see. There was an oilcloth on the table, though. And there was a piece of charred wood in the stove. I got it out, still warm, and wrote on the oilcloth: *Thanks. I'm going back with a U.S. marshal that believes I didn't do nothing wrong. I'll come see you when I get turned loose. Your obedient servant.* I signed it *Jason.*

I put the charcoal back in the stove and wiped my hand on my pants. Why any girl would of helped me, I couldn't know. I was dirty and smelly and my hair was like the mangy hair of an animal. But she had believed me and helped me and that put a kind of warm feeling in my belly. If I got out of the trouble I was in, I sure did mean to come back here and thank her proper for what she'd done. She'd kept me from being caught by Sligh and Donahue and Sheriff Bidwell, who would've joined up just as soon as Donahue and Bidwell caught up with Sligh.

We went out. The marshal mounted first and gave me a stirrup and I swung up behind him. He turned the horse and put him into a trot, heading for Cheyenne.

Well, I guess we didn't leave soon enough, or else

Jessie's pa hadn't been very far away. We'd no more topped the first rise after leaving the sod shack before we looked behind and seen dust raising from three horsemen riding toward us.

Marshal Rittenhouse said, "Looks like we're in for it, boy. Hang on." He sank spurs into his horse's sides and the big animal dug in and ran. I put my arms around the marshal's waist and hung on. He was thick and solid and as hard as iron and I figured if anybody could fight off three like Sligh and Donahue and Sheriff Bidwell, he could.

We rode like this for several miles. The horse was heating up and sweating. He was steamy under me and his neck was wet with sweat. I yelled, "How long you reckon he can run like this?"

"Not much longer. I'm looking for a place we can stop and hold 'em off!"

There wasn't no such place, but all of a sudden I seen a kind of line along the horizon up ahead. The marshal must of seen it at the same time because he pointed. "See that? Ought to be someplace there we could hole up."

It turned out, as we got closer, that the line I'd seen was a bluff maybe fifty or sixty feet high. Up at the top the rock dropped off straight down for twenty feet and from there it was a steep and rocky slope to the prairie.

It took us near an hour to reach it. I saw that there was some scrub piñons up on top of the rim. Marshal Rittenhouse picked himself a gully and followed it all the way up to the rim. He got off, and hoisted me down, and then led the horse on up a steep trail through the rim. We had a good view of the prairie and them chasing us, and if they tried to come on us from behind, we had them scrubby trees to give us cover. I figured we was lucky to of found a place like this.

Donahue and Sligh and Sheriff Bidwell galloped right up to the foot of the bluff. They stopped and sat their horses looking up toward where we was. They talked amongst themselves for a long time, once in a while pointing up toward us.

Finally they got off their horses. Sligh stayed down there at the foot of the slide. Sheriff Bidwell headed off toward the right and Mr. Donahue toward the left. They figured to get us in a crossfire from three sides and fix it so's we couldn't get away.

I looked at the marshal's face. He didn't look scared and he didn't look worried. He said, "Keep your head down, kid."

Being a law officer, I guess he didn't feel like he could start shooting first. So we waited, and pretty soon a gun boomed off on our right, followed by one on our left. Both bullets cut twigs from the piñons. Right afterward, Sligh fired from the bottom of the slide. I don't know where his bullet went, but I figured it was fired wild on purpose. Donahue and Sheriff Bidwell might want me dead but Sligh didn't. He wanted me alive.

Marshal Rittenhouse took careful aim on the rock Sligh was hiding behind down at the foot of the bluff and fired. The bullet struck just as Sligh raised his head. He ducked back real quick and I figured he had been showered with rock pieces broken off by the bullet striking right in front of him.

He didn't poke his head up again. Sheriff Bidwell yelled, "Marshal, you're interferin' with a law officer in the performance of his duty. Turn that boy over to us."

Marshal Rittenhouse didn't even answer that. They fired again and cut some more twigs out of the piñons but he was watching for their powdersmoke and he fired almost right away. I heard Sheriff Bidwell yell, as if he'd been nicked, and I saw Marshal Rittenhouse grin.

He swung around now and stared toward where Donahue was hid, his eyes squinting against the sinking sun. I said, "What we going to do?"

He said, "It's going to be dark pretty soon. Soon's it is, we'll get away all right."

I hoped he was right, and I had to admit it was a doggone good feeling to have somebody on my side. Mr. Hunnicutt had been on my side, but he was dead, and the girl, Jessie, had been on my side, but she hadn't been able to do anything. I figured Marshal Rittenhouse was different. He didn't seem worried to be surrounded by three men desperate enough to kill us both.

Pretty soon Donahue stuck his head up and the marshal fired, and grinned. Donahue hadn't been hit because he didn't yell, but I guess the bullet had come close enough to scare the hell out of him.

After that, there wasn't no more shooting. The sun settled down in the west and finally sank behind the horizon. The clouds was bright pink and orange and gold for a spell, and then the sky turned gray.

The three surrounding us opened up again, but they was shooting wild because they didn't want to let themselves be seen. It got darker and darker and pretty soon Marshal Rittenhouse was able to shoot at the flashes of their guns. I hoped they wouldn't just happen to hit his horse because that would leave us out here afoot, but I guess we was lucky, because the horse wasn't hit.

Soon as it was real dark, Marshal Rittenhouse shot at

all three of them in turn and then he said, "Come on, kid. We're leaving here."

I followed him to where the horse was tied in that thick clump of piñon pines. He untied him and mounted and then put down a hand and helped me up. He rode out at a slow walk, leaning forward and stroking his horse's muzzle, ready to clamp his hand over his nostrils if he smelled one of them other horses. He didn't, though, and pretty soon we was far enough away so's Mr. Rittenhouse figured he could let the horse trot.

There was a few more shots behind, but when they wasn't answered, the three must of figured we was gone. Pretty soon we heard the sound of horses galloping. Mr. Rittenhouse stopped his horse and clamped his hand over the horse's nostrils and we waited there until the galloping had gone on past. Marshal Rittenhouse said, "We ain't going to see them again until Cheyenne."

We didn't, neither. We rode to Cheyenne at a steady trot. It was bouncy but I was able to doze off a few times, only waking up when I commenced to topple off.

We came into Cheyenne just as the sky was getting light. Sure enough, they was waiting for us. They opened up with a volley of shots as we crossed the railroad tracks. One of the bullets went right into the chest of the marshal's horse. He went to his knees, then laid down on one side, wheezing and bubbling. I jumped clear and streaked for the railroad station. The marshal wasn't far behind.

Bullets kicked up dust and ricocheted off the steel railroad tracks. But we reached the station building before either of us got hit. I didn't know what the marshal was going to do, but I figured he knew better what to do than me. I waited to see what he would say.

CHAPTER 20

There was an agent in the station. He poked his head out to see what was going on, but yanked it back real quick when a bullet hitting the station stung him with splinters. His face was as white and scared as any I've ever seen. I reckon he crawled under the counter because we didn't see him again.

I didn't have no gun, and I wasn't sure I'd of used it anyway. I'd never been in no gunbattle with no one and you never know until it happens what you'll do and how you'll act. The marshal kept throwing shots around the corner of the railroad depot and finally he said, "Kid, we'd better get up to the judge's house."

I thought that would be a good idea, but I didn't see how we was going to manage it. I nodded and he stuck his head out and yelled, "Sligh! This boy ain't going to do you no good dead. You keep them fellows busy long enough for us to get away and you got a chance. Don't, and they'll have the Hunnicutt ranch and you'll have a piece of paper that ain't no good to anyone."

He waited just a minute for that to sink in, then he said, "Come on," and I followed him away from the railroad station and down the tracks.

Back behind us I heard some yelling and some shots and I figured Sligh had done what the marshal said. He was keeping Mr. Donahue and Sheriff Bidwell pinned down long enough for us to get away.

We ran along the tracks for a couple of hundred yards until the marshal figured we was out of range. Then we cut in toward town. We kept to alleys and side streets and people's yards until we finally made it to the part of town where all the important people lived. Mr. Rittenhouse seemed to know the town and where the judge's house was, so I guessed he'd been here before. After what seemed a long time to me, we slowed down and went through a white picket gate and walked up the gravel path to a big, three-story white house, shining in the morning sun. Mr. Rittenhouse twisted the bell on the door and pretty soon a woman came and Marshal Rittenhouse said, "Marshal Rittenhouse to see Judge Whitaker, ma'am. Please tell him that we're here."

I kept looking around for Donahue and Sheriff Bidwell, and I seen them turn the corner and come up the street. They wasn't riding their horses, but was kind of trotting along on foot. I said, "Marshal, there they are."

He glanced around. The woman had gone to tell the judge we was here, but Marshal Rittenhouse didn't wait for her to come back. He pushed me into the house and followed, closing the door behind. He peered out through the glass in the upper part of the door and I stood there shivering. The house smelled like the one out at the Hunnicutt ranch, of thick rugs, and padded furniture and good food that had been cooked the night before.

Pretty soon the judge, wearing a nightshirt and a robe, came along the hall. He looked cross as he said, "What is the meaning of this?"

Marshal Rittenhouse said, "Judge, Red Donahue and

Sheriff Bidwell are trying to kill this boy. And me too."

"He's an escaped criminal. Take him down to the jail and bring him to court at ten o'clock."

He wasn't giving even a little bit and it looked like I was right back where I'd been a couple of days ago. The marshal said, "Judge, I've talked to several members of the Hunnicutt crew. I don't think this boy's done anything worse than be in the wrong place at the wrong time. Donahue killed Mr. Hunnicutt because he got caught upstairs with Mr. Hunnicutt's wife."

"You can substantiate this?"

"Yes, sir, Judge. This here boy's dirty and he looks pretty scraggly, but he's only a boy and he wouldn't kill nobody, least of all a man who's befriended him."

The judge frowned for a long, long time. The marshal said, "They ambushed us down at the railroad station as we rode into town, and they're out there right now waiting to kill us when we come out."

"What do you want me to do?" asked the judge.

"Well, sir, if you'll issue warrants for the arrest of Sheriff Bidwell and Donahue, I can serve them because I'm a U.S. marshal and I'll put them down in the jail."

"What about this boy?"

"Well, Judge, if he was to be cleaned up, he'd likely have a lot better chance of getting a fair trial, now wouldn't he?"

"You mean you want me to keep him here?"

"It's the only place I know of where he'll be safe until them two varmints are in jail."

The judge scowled at me for a long time but finally nodded his head. He called, "Mrs. Chavez!"

The woman came and the judge said, "Take this boy and

see that he gets a bath. Cut his hair and whiskers if you can. Then give him something to eat. He's supposed to be in court at ten."

I guessed she didn't like the job because she looked at me like I was some kind of animal. The judge said, "He's near my size, so give him some of my clothes to wear."

She said something that sounded like "mumpff," but she said, "Come on," and led me up the stairs. There was a room with a fancy bathtub and a porcelain pot in it, and she told me to get my stinking clothes off and she'd bring water and some others for me to put on when I was through. I took off my clothes and stood there shivering until I heard her coming, and then I grabbed them up and covered myself the best I could because it wasn't decent for a strange woman to see me naked, no matter how old she was.

She came in and poured two pails of water into the tub and said, "Get in and wash. I'll bring more water for you to rinse."

It seemed funny, but I got in the tub. There was soap and I washed, and pretty soon the water was dirty gray. She came up and dumped a pail of cold water over me and I got out of the tub, shivering, as soon as she'd left again. I dried and by the time I'd finished, she was there with some clothes of the judge's that I could put on. When I'd finished dressing, she came with a razor and scissors and she shaved me and cut my hair, muttering disapprovingly all the time.

She drained out the bathtub just by pulling a plug. There was a pipe from the bathtub on outside someplace. I followed her downstairs. The judge was there, dressed and ready to go to court. He said, "It wouldn't look right for you to come to court with me. I suppose the marshal will be coming back for you as soon as he's through jailing Mr. Donahue and Sheriff Bidwell."

I said, "Yes, sir."

He looked closely at me. "I hope this will be a lesson to you."

I said, "Yes, sir." It would be. If I ever got up to go to the outhouse in the middle of the night again and heard a shot, I'd go back to bed and pull the covers up over my head.

I sat down in a velvet-covered chair. The judge went out, but pretty soon the doorbell rang and Mrs. Chavez answered it and it was Marshal Rittenhouse. He said, "Come on, kid. You ought to be out of the woods."

I said, "Yes, sir," and followed him. We walked down the street toward the courthouse and he said, "I got Sheriff Bidwell and Donahue locked up in jail. I'll take you to court, and then I'll go fetch them."

I didn't think to ask him about Sligh. The marshal took me to the courthouse and into the courtroom, where he left me with the bailiff of the court, a little, dried-up man with gold-rimmed spectacles. I sat down and waited. Pretty soon the marshal came back with Donahue and Sheriff Bidwell, both of them handcuffed.

The bailiff said, "The District Court of the County of Laramie, Territory of Wyoming, is now in session. Judge William J. Whitaker presiding. All rise."

The judge came in and everybody stood up and the bailiff said, "Be seated."

Everybody sat down and the judge pounded on his bench with a gavel and he said, "Call the case of Jason Ord."

The bailiff said, "Case of the people of the Territory of

Wyoming versus Jason Ord. Charge is murder in the first degree."

The judge looked at the marshal. "Take the stand, Marshal Rittenhouse."

The prosecutor got up. "This is highly irregular."

The judge said, "Sit down, Mr. Savage. Marshal Rittenhouse is in possession of new facts concerning this case."

Marshal Rittenhouse took the stand. He told the judge what he had told him earlier. I didn't know how he'd done it, but he had Ike, the blacksmith at the Hunnicutt ranch, and a couple of others waiting to testify. They was called, and they told what they knew, and when it was all finished, the judge looked at the prosecutor and asked him to approach the bench, along with the lawyer that had been representing me. They talked for a while and pretty soon the judge said, "The state has agreed to dismiss the charges against Jason Ord. The prosecutor's office will file a charge of murder in the first degree against Mr. Donahue. He will file a charge of malfeasance in office against Sheriff Bidwell. The defendant is released from custody."

I couldn't hardly believe my ears. Marshal Rittenhouse came over to me and shook my hand. He said, "The judge is going to study that will, Jason; but chances are that it will stand up. How's it going to feel, owning a ranch as big as Hunnicutt's?"

I said, "I don't own it yet. It feels good enough for me just to be free again."

He shook my hand. "Good luck. I'll stay around until the Cheyenne marshal gets back and then I'll be going along."

I said, "Marshal, thanks sounds pretty weak."

He said, "It's enough, and you're welcome, boy. Good luck to you."

He went out. I stood there all alone, hardly able to believe that I was really free. Maybe I owned the Hunnicutt ranch, but I didn't have two cents in my pockets and no place to stay. Still, being free was enough for now. I'd slept out before and I'd gone hungry, and I could again. I went out into the morning sunlight and it sure hadn't felt so warm and good before.

I don't know why I'd forgotten him, but I had. Only Sligh hadn't forgotten me. He still had the paper I'd been forced to sign, giving him a share in the Hunnicutt ranch, and giving him all of it if I was dead.

I didn't think about Sligh, or remember him, and although I didn't know it, I was safe until the judge ruled on Mr. Hunnicutt's will. Suddenly I saw Jessie and she came over to me and said, "I'm glad."

I said, "I didn't get no chance to thank you proper, ma'am. But I surely do."

"I didn't help you."

I said, "You sure did lead Donahue and Sheriff Bidwell away. I reckon you saved my life is all."

She said, "I want you to meet my pa."

I shook hands with her pa, a tough-looking, gray-haired man. I said, "The marshal says I'll likely inherit the Hunnicutt ranch."

She said, "Then you'll likely want no more to do with the likes of us."

I said, "I ain't never likely to feel that way about folks that has been friends to me."

Her pa said, "Let's all go eat."

We went to a restaurant and ate and he paid for it.

When we came out, Jessie's pa and her said they had to go. They got in a buggy and drove out of town after I'd promised I'd come see Jessie first chance I got.

I went back to the courthouse. Near one o'clock, I met the judge coming back for the afternoon session of his court. Before I could open my mouth, he said, "I've looked over that will of Mr. Hunnicutt's. I think it's a true will and I'm going to rule that it's valid. You own the Hunnicutt ranch, Jason Ord."

I guess I was kind of stunned. I'd never owned nothing in my whole life and now I owned one of the biggest ranches hereabouts. I walked out into the street in a daze. I still didn't think about Sligh. I should of, though. He was in that courtroom when the judge called it to order and he heard the judge's first pronouncement, which was that the Hunnicutt will leaving everything to me was valid and would be upheld. First thing he done was to come looking for me. He knew that with me dead, he'd own it all, or at least him and Rousch would and he could worry about gettin' rid of Rousch later on.

CHAPTER 21

I stood out in front of the courthouse for a long time, just soaking up the sun and feeling warm. There was a kind of excitement in thinking about owning the Hunnicutt ranch. But it scared me too. I wasn't big enough or old enough or smart enough to run it right. I guessed I'd have to ask the crew to help me out and maybe hire somebody who was older and smarter to be the foreman of it. I thought about Jessie's pa and guessed he'd be a good one for that job if he'd take it.

Well, it was time I stopped standing around wondering what to do. First thing was to go to the livery stable and hire a horse. Then I'd ride out to the Hunnicutt ranch.

I headed for the stable. I just happened to look around from half a block away and I saw Sligh coming down the courthouse steps. He hurried up when he saw me, and I began to run. As I turned the first corner I looked behind. He was running too.

I guess I could have circled around and gone back to the courthouse, but I was so scared I didn't think of it. Sligh had beaten me bad once, and he'd tried to beat me a second time. Now he only wanted the ranch, but he wanted to even the score for the knot I'd put on his head last time he tried beating me. He'd beat me to death this time because that was the way he wanted me.

Scared as I was, I knowed one thing for sure. Running wasn't no good this time. I'd tried running before and Sligh always caught up to me. He had the paper I'd signed giving him an interest in the Hunnicutt ranch, and he'd follow me out there even if I was able to get away from him here in town.

No, sir. This time I was going to have to fight Sligh, and he had a gun and I didn't and that didn't give me too much chance unless I could get my hands on one.

But where? I was running like a rabbit now, figuring I was faster on my feet than Sligh. I cut right real hard and suddenly I found myself on the main street of Cheyenne where all the business houses was. Down there about a block away there was a saloon and out in front of it horses was tied to the rail and on one of them I seen a rifle stock sticking up out of a saddle boot. If I could get my hands on that gun, and if it was loaded, I figured I'd have a chance.

One thing was in my favor. Sligh wouldn't dare murder me in plain sight of other people because if he did, he'd have to pay for it. Sligh had to get me away from people so's he could do me in without there being any witnesses.

On the other hand, if he could get his hands on me, he sure could drag me away to wherever he wanted to do me in. Or I'd just plain disappear. If I wasn't never found, nobody could say he killed me and nobody could keep him from taking over the Hunnicutt ranch.

So I kept running. Just before I reached the horse with the rifle sticking up out of a saddle boot, I slowed down and walked. Looking behind, I seen that Sligh was only about a quarter block away. I didn't have much time, and I didn't dare steal the horse because if I did a commotion would go up and I'd sure get myself caught.

I walked out between the horses. I looked up and down to see if anybody was watching me. Nobody seemed to be, so I reached up and snatched the rifle out of the boot.

Somebody said, "Hey! Hey, you! Put that rifle back!"

I didn't look to see who it was. I ran across the street, just getting barely missed by a team and buckboard rattling down the street. Behind me I heard the same voice yell, "Hey you! Stop!"

I didn't stop. I ducked between two buildings and ran along a passageway that wasn't no wider than a foot and a half. There was trash and tin cans, and once I almost fell. Looking back, I seen Sligh come into the passageway just as I was leaving it.

I'd stolen something and in the eyes of the law I was a thief, and that gave Sligh the right to shoot me, and the other man who'd owned the rifle, and I figured Sligh would try and see to it that the other man done his killing for him. It would work, if they caught up with me. I couldn't shoot the man who'd owned the gun even to save myself.

But I was getting mad, like I had a couple of times before. All I wanted was to be left alone and I hadn't done nothing wrong except just now to steal that rifle out of the man's saddle boot. I'd been pushed around enough, and by the Lord I'd been hounded enough, and I wasn't going to take no more of it.

Sligh shot at me just as I ducked out of the end of the passageway and I heard the bullet strike a tin can near the alley and send it rolling and clattering.

There was a stairway leading up to a second story of one of the buildings and even knowing I'd be cornered up there, I took it, two steps at a time. I was at the top and crouched down behind the railing when Sligh come busting out of the passageway with the other man right behind. The other man stopped and said, "Where'd he go?"

Sligh was looking around, but he didn't look up. He said, "The little sonofabitch!"

The other man said, "What'd he do? Why you chasin' him?"

Sligh said, "Just wanta talk to him is all. Him an' me just inherited a ranch."

"Then why you shootin' at him?"

"He stole your gun, didn't he? That kid's dangerous. He's a bad 'un an' he'll use that gun if he gets the chance."

The other man said, "You settle it. If you get my gun back, I'll be in the saloon."

Sligh said, "Sure enough." The other man went back into the passageway and Sligh kept standing there.

I held my breath. If he looked up . . . He had a reason for killing me now. I was armed and he'd told that man I was dangerous. If he shot me he could claim it was in self-defense. It might sound pretty thin, but who could prove otherwise?

He walked slowly across the trash-littered yard. There was a ramshackle stable back near the alley and he went toward it like a cat stalking a bird. I had to breathe. I'd been holding my breath too long.

I let it out slowly, so as not to make too much noise. I needn't of worried because just then I heard someone coming along the passageway, kicking tin cans out of the way.

Sligh whirled around, but the man who came out of the passageway was Rousch, the lawyer Sligh had hired in Denver. Sligh said, "Well, I'm glad to see you here. The judge gave the kid that ranch, just like I said he would.

Now the kid's loose somewheres and he's got a gun he stole."

Rousch said, "Well, if he's a thief and has got a gun, then anybody would say he's dangerous. I guess that gives us the right to kill him when we catch up to him."

Sligh grinned at him. He said, "That's just the way I figured it. You might say we're actin' on behalf of the law, you being a lawyer and all."

I wished there was a hole I could crawl into but there wasn't. Sooner or later, one of them two would look up. They must feel me staring down at them because I was so damn' scared.

And sure enough, they did. Both of them looked up at the same time, and seen me squatted down there behind that rail. Sligh raised his gun and fired almost without thinking and something slammed into my leg. It felt like a mule kicking me and it sent me sprawling back across that stairway landing and into the wall behind. I didn't hardly believe what had happened, but the blood running out of my leg and soaking the judge's pants was something nobody could disbelieve.

Sligh yelled, "I got him, by God. Let's go up and finish the little bastard off!"

The two ran toward the bottom of the stairway, and I heard them pounding up the stairs. I hadn't looked close at the gun I'd stole before, and now I looked down at it. If it wasn't loaded, I was dead. Soon as Sligh hit the top of the stairs, he'd kill me and that would be the end of Jason Ord.

It was a lever action gun, a repeater, and I worked the lever, staring down into the breech as I did. My lips was moving and I was saying, "Oh God, help me out. Have there be ca'tridges in this here gun!"

I seen something that looked like brass, but there wasn't no time for making sure. Sligh was almost to the top of the stairs and Rousch right behind, and I was plumb out of time. I closed the action and raised the gun. If it clicked on an empty, that was the end for Jason Ord.

I seen Sligh's head poke up above the landing, but I didn't shoot. I figured real quick that I'd better wait for a bigger target than his head.

I seen his gun as he came on up, and I thought, Now! and pulled the trigger of the gun. It bucked hard against me, and the bullet must of slammed right into Mr. Sligh's chest because he fell back, and I heard Mr. Rousch yell as Sligh hit him and knocked him on down the stairs.

But Rousch didn't waste no time after he recovered from the surprise. He grabbed Mr. Sligh's gun and he come on up the stairs after me. I was ready this time and I knowed the gun was loaded. When he poked Sligh's gun on above the landing, I was ready and when his chest appeared, I fired the gun again.

He disappeared and I heard him rolling down the stairs.

That was both of them, I thought. My head was whirling and I felt dizzy, and I guessed I was going to die. But by God, I'd fought back, and even if I died, I had the satisfaction of knowing that I had.

There was a lot of yelling, and a big crowd of people crowded through the passageway. I used what was left of my strength and threw the rifle away from me so when they came up the stairs they wouldn't finish me off. I heard it hit the ground down below and I knowed that if I didn't bleed to death, maybe I'd be safe at last.

Well, I was almost out, but I felt hands lifting me, and I heard voices all mixed up, and when I woke up again I was in a bed in somebody's house and Jessie and her pa and the marshal was all looking down at me. The marshal said, "Well, I'm glad you finally decided to wake up."

Jessie was crying. I said, "What about them two?"

The marshal said, "Well, we found the papers they made you sign on them. I reckon there'll be an inquest, but it don't look like nobody can be blamed much for just defending theirselves."

The marshal looked at Jessie's pa. "Why don't I buy you a drink?"

Jessie's pa looked kind of doubtful, but Jessie said, "It's all right, Pa."

Him and the marshal left. Jessie sat there for a while. Finally she said, "You likely think I'm forward, but I hope I'm going to see you again."

I said, "You are." I reached out a hand and took hers and she smiled at me and I figured that finally things was going to be all right. Nobody was out to kill me no more and it looked like maybe I'd found somebody who cared what happened to me, and who might go on caring for a long, long time to come.